THE MACARON WITCH

BROOMSTICK BAKERY #2

LAURA GREENWOOD

BLURB

When Hazel is invited to teach a cooking class on magic imbibed macarons, the last thing she expects is to meet a handsome sous chef who sweeps her off her feet.

Antonio has always felt like he's living in his father's shadow, but now there's a gorgeous witch who seems to see him for who he really is, and he's determined not to let her slip away.

They soon discover that the sparks flying between them aren't just in the kitchen...

-

The Macaron Witch is a paranormal romance and part of the Broomstick Bakery series. It includes witchy bakers, enchanted patisserie, and a standalone m/f romance.

ONE

HAZEL

THE BUILDING in front of me appears unchanged since my days as a cookery student here. I don't think there's a single part of it that's different. I suppose that's what happens when you attend an education facility that's mostly aimed at witches.

And I'm here to teach a class. It's a surreal feeling and a small part of me is wondering what I was thinking when I said yes to this. I'm not a teacher, I'm just a twenty-something patissier who runs a family bakery with my three sisters.

It doesn't seem like yesterday that I was here

learning how to make the perfect frosting, or the most delicious puff pastry.

Not that I'm the best at the last one, pastry is more Clover's forté than mine, and I often find myself reaching out to my older sister to make me some when I need it. We always work as a team to make sure the items on display in the shop are the best we can possibly manage.

No one pays any attention to me as I make my way through the crowded corridors. I imagine I probably look just like any other student. Perhaps I shouldn't have left my hair a shocking shade of blue this morning.

I reach up to touch it. I could go to the bathroom and change it, but I dismiss the notion. If the students I'm here to teach aren't going to take me seriously, then that's on them.

I head straight to the front desk and put on my best smile. "Hi, I'm Hazel Parkes, I think you're expecting me."

She nods. "Let me check."

I shift from one foot to the other while I wait for her to pull up the right information on the screen.

"Ah, yes. Chef DeRossi is waiting for you in demonstration room C. Do you need directions?" she asks.

"No, thank you, I studied here."

"Go right through, I'll let Chef know you're here." She picks up a phone, which I take as my cue to leave.

I head down one of the corridors and come to demonstration room C. I pause for a moment, wondering whether I should knock. In the end, I push the door open and step inside.

My heart skips a beat at the sight of the man I've looked up to for the past ten years. I can't believe I'm about to meet him. I was gutted when the news came that he'd taken over running the cookery school just two years after I left.

I clear my throat. "Hi, I'm Hazel Parkes, I'm here for the guest demonstration," I say.

Blood pounds in my ear as I wait for him to tell me that this has all been a huge mistake and I've not been invited to speak at all.

But when he turns to face me, I can see a friendly smile on his face. "Ah, yes, I've been expecting you," he responds in barely accented English. "I'm Chef DeRossi."

A small squeak threatens to break free from me, but I squash it down. Now isn't the time for me to start fangirling, but it's hard not to when he's one of the foremost pastry chefs in the world as well as my idol.

"We're looking forward to your class today," he

says. "I've heard great things about your magic-infused baking."

"Thank you. It's a family tradition going back several generations," I say needlessly. He knows that, it's why he asked for me to come and speak about this in the first place.

He nods and gestures for me to follow him. "Everything you requested for your demonstration is waiting for you. I trust you know how to use all of the equipment?"

"I do. I was a student here just before you took over."

"Aha, so that is why your pastries are so delicious."

"You've had one of them?" Is this really happening? I wish Clover was here to pinch me, because I'm not sure this isn't a dream.

"Of course. I wouldn't invite anyone whose food I have not tasted to speak here."

It's a fair rule, and one I'd probably employ if I ran a cookery school.

A dark-haired man steps into the room wearing classic chef whites. He seems around my age, though that could mean anything from early-twenties to mid-forties, and has a similar complexion to Chef DeRossi. Perhaps he's also Italian.

"This is my sous-chef, Antonio," Chef DeRossi says as he gestures towards the man.

Antonio smiles at me and holds out his hand. I take it and shake firmly, trying to focus on something other than how well my hand fits in his.

"It's a pleasure to meet you," I say.

"Likewise."

"I'm Hazel."

"Antonio," he says needlessly, only then dropping my hand. But it doesn't feel like it's been some kind of power-play, more like he forgot he was holding you.

"Antonio will be assisting you with your class," Chef DeRossi says. "He'll be ensuring everything runs smoothly."

"Oh, I didn't realise I needed an assistant." If I had, I'd have asked one of my sisters to come, and if they'd been busy, I'm sure my brother would have skipped a day of academy to come down and help me out.

Not that I'm allowed to ask him to do that according to Mum and Dad.

"I'll leave the two of you to it," DeRossi says with a dip of his head, already heading towards the door.

"Great, thank you," I murmur.

I glance around the room, taking it all in and

trying to reconcile what I'm seeing with the idea of a dozen students coming into the room in about an hour.

"I guess we'd better get started," I say.

Antonio flashes me a reassuring smile. "Just tell me what you want me to do, I'm all yours for the afternoon."

His accent gives the words *I'm all yours* a delightful flirtiness to them that I'm not sure he meant to be there. I'm going to have to be on my guard with him.

"Do you mind if I start making the batch of macarons I need?" I ask.

"Be my guest." He gestures to the demonstration bench at the front. "It will be useful for me to see how you work and how I can assist you best. It'll also let me set up the cameras better."

"Cameras?" I squeak slightly as I ask.

He nods. "So the students can see what you're doing more closely."

"Oh, right. Of course." I smile, trying to hide my apprehension about the entire setup. I've attended plenty of demonstrations like this over the years, I know what they're like and how important it is to make sure everyone has a good view.

Neither of us says anything as I start making my

macarons and he sets up the equipment, but it isn't an uncomfortable silence, even when I catch him looking at what I'm doing with interest.

"Have you worked with Chef DeRossi for long?" I ask as I pipe out my batch of macarons to rest.

"Ever since I left college," he admits. "He's a great chef."

"He is. I learned a lot from the online masterclass he did a couple of years back."

"You attended that?"

"You seem surprised?"

"It's just that I read up on you when I learned you were coming here to teach a class, and you sound like you're very successful."

I laugh uneasily. "I wouldn't call myself *very* successful. I'm lucky enough to have inherited a bakery from my grandmother." Along with my three older sisters.

"And you turned it from a local bread shop into a shop that's known for miles around."

I reach up and tuck a strand of hair behind my ear before realising I shouldn't be touching it and going to wash my hands.

"I suppose that's true. We've made a name for ourselves. But I'm not sure why it surprises you that I took DeRossi's masterclass."

He shrugs. "I wouldn't have thought you needed it."

"How can I be the best if I don't learn from the best?" I ask. "I have to keep up to date on the techniques the leaders in the field of patisserie are using, that way I can adapt my recipes and make sure they're truly the best things I can create."

"I hadn't looked at it that way," he admits.

"But you probably go to a restaurant and look at the menu and the plates and consider how they've put everything together and if there's something you can learn from them, right?"

"Well, yes."

I cock my head to the side and study him intently. "How is that any different?"

A contemplative expression crosses his face, as if he's never stopped to wonder about it. "You have a point."

"I know." I grin widely. "Do you mind if I use my wand to set a timer?" I'm not sure why he would, but it's polite to ask.

"Be my guest."

I pull it from my pocket and wave it towards the air so a timer pops up. After a moment's consideration, I pull up another one so I know how long I have until my class begins. The last thing I want is to be caught off guard and not be ready when they come in.

Nerves start to build, but I focus on the task at hand. Making macarons always soothes me, and today is no different than any other in that regard. I just have to make sure everything is perfect.

TWO

HAZEL

NERVES FILL me as I face a room full of people who are eager to learn what I have to teach. Why did I think this was a good idea? I've never taught anyone to do anything before, and now I'm up here about to reveal family secrets to everyone watching.

I take a deep breath. My sisters approved of this idea, and even if I teach people what to do, it doesn't mean that they'll become our competitors. The world is big enough for more than one bakery.

I glance at Antonio, who gives me a small smile and a nod. I like him. He seems to be aware that this is difficult for me, but doesn't question my ability.

I've met plenty of other chefs who would have laughed me out of the kitchen thanks to my basic training and the fact I work at a bakery and not in a restaurant.

"Good afternoon," I say brightly, forcing a smile onto my face. "I'm Hazel Parkes, and I'm here to show you the best process for imbibing magic into your patisserie. We're going to start with macarons." I debated choosing something easier when I came up with my lesson plan, but these really show off the best way that I can do it.

I check my workbench to make sure everything is in position, including my wand. When it comes to making meringues, timing is everything, and I don't want to be reaching for something only to find it's not where it should be.

"We're going to start with a standard recipe for macarons. Don't touch your wands until I tell you it's time." I feel bossy even saying it, but I know it's the right instruction to give.

With Antonio's help, I start the process of making the macaron shells, narrating the steps as I go, though I doubt many of the people in this class really need me to do it. The icing sugar and almonds go in first, mixed well and then sieved. I add two of the egg whites in and set them to the side while I focus on the rest.

"I personally like to use a thermometer for my sugar syrup," I say as I drop one in with the water and sugar that's starting to simmer away. "But if you prefer to use a spell to alert you when it's at one-hundred-and-ten degrees, then that's also okay."

Antonio clears his throat and I nod at him, realising he probably wants to say something that'll help the students. "If you do use a spell, please keep in mind that there are multiple people in the room and it shouldn't be too intrusive," he says.

I nod and make a mental note to say something like that if I ever need to teach anyone again.

"If you're imbibing your macarons with pixie dust, you need to add it in with the sugar now." After a lot of experimenting, that's where it does best. Something about the way pixie dust melts is akin to sugar. Not that it's ever my choice of ingredient to do that.

None of the students add anything.

"Once the syrup is at a hundred-and-ten, you should start whisking your eggs." I keep an eye on my thermometer, not wanting my demonstration to go badly because I'm not paying enough attention. Perhaps I should have used a spell, but I don't like the way it can interfere with the bake.

A quick glance at the students in front of me reveals that almost all of them are doing the same thing I am, though I'm not sure if it's because they prefer it, or if they just think that following my lead is the best example.

With the syrup almost done, I start my electric stand whisk to start beating the eggs. I don't want to confuse anyone by mentioning this part can be done with magic too, in fact, my sister Oakley would be doing it that way. But this is my class, so I'm going to make the macarons the way I like to.

"Once your sugar reaches one-hundred-and-eighteen degrees, you need to pour it down the side of your mixing bowl, but be careful not to hit the whisk." My heart pounds as I do what I've just described. Somehow, this is more nerve-wracking than any other time I've made macarons.

I take a steadying breath. I've done this hundreds of times, I'm not going to mess it up just because people are watching me now.

"You should continue whisking the mixture until it's cooled down and you can see shiny peaks form. The bowl should be *warm* to touch, but should not be hot." I lean in to check my own bowl, relieved to find that it's exactly as I describe it to be. "This is when you should add colour into your bowl, and if you're adding a flavour to your macaron shells, this is when you should do that too." Though it's not the most advisable to.

I pick up my wand and tap the side of the bowl once, turning the mixture into the same bright shade of blue as my hair. I've used food colouring before, but I don't think it's anywhere near as vibrant when the bake is complete.

Some of the students do the same with their wands, while others use more traditional methods of colouring. The whirr of stand mixers fills the air as they all make sure their colours are spread through the mixture well.

"Once you're satisfied that your colour is mixed in, you need to fold the meringue mixture into your almond one. Be sure not to go too far or your macarons won't turn out too well. The mixture should fall back into the bowl as a ribbon and disappear within thirty seconds." I hold up my spatula and let the mix fall off in order to demonstrate, dimly aware of the screen behind giving a close up of what I'm doing.

Just another reminder that I can't get this wrong. I wish I'd taken the option to pre-record my lesson instead of giving it live.

"Once that's done, you need to turn your oven on to one-hundred-and-seventy degrees to let it preheat. Now we're going to pipe the macarons. Your nozzle should be about a centimetre away from the baking sheet, and your macarons should be about two point five centimetres round. You can use a macaron mat if you prefer to help. They'll need to rest for about thirty minutes prior to baking, and should have a skin on them before they go into the oven."

My hands shake as I start to pipe the confections. I shouldn't be reacting this way, but with everyone watching me, it's hard to stay calm.

I glance at Antonio, who seems to be watching me with a rapt fascination that seems to be very little to do with making sure he removes the equipment that could otherwise get in my way.

"All right, while we're waiting, we need to clear up our workstations. We'll need the space to make the filling and to prep the rest of the shells. When the timer goes off, we need to put our macarons in the oven." With a flick of my wand, I conjure a timer in the air above all of our heads. Ideally, I like macarons to rest for longer than half an hour just to be on the safe side, but with the limited time available for a class, I don't want to risk it.

Though now I'm saying it, I realise that there's not a lot to actually clean up thanks to Antonio.

A soft din of chatter fills the room as the students start talking about what they've just learned while tidying up and putting their dirty pots in the many dishwashers spread around the side of the room.

"You're doing well," Antonio says softly.

I give him a wary smile. "Thank you. Am I not talking too fast?"

He shakes his head. "You're explaining clearly. But I did think you'd put magic into every part of the recipe."

"Oh no, you don't want to do that. It ends up being overwhelming and drowning out all of your other emotions and feelings for too long. People do some dumb things when they can't feel fear and sadness."

"I never realised that was such an issue. So that's how you decide what to put in?"

"And how much. The effects of the macaron will wear off after about an hour, and it won't drown out the rest of your emotions between now and then. But whether it takes at all depends on the person putting the magic in. It's a lot more intense than other spells."

He bobs his head along with what I'm saying, as if he's filing it away for use later. "It surprises me that more people don't do it."

I shrug. "Me too. Maybe it's the fear of getting it wrong? There are laws in place about when and where it can be used and they're a bit complicated."

"Do you need a licence in order to sell the cakes like this?" He gestures to the drying macaron shells.

"No, but I think you should."

He quirks an eyebrow but doesn't say anything to contradict me. I can understand that. It's a controversial thing to say when I make my living by selling emotion infused patisserie.

But it's something that can be dangerous in the wrong hands, and I'd be very foolish not to appreciate that.

The timer goes off, and the students return to their positions behind their workbenches.

"All right, your macarons should now have a skin on them," I say, pointing to my own in order to demonstrate. "And it's time for them to go in the oven for fourteen minutes."

I flick my wand at the timer again, instantly resetting it to the right time. Hopefully, the ovens in the training kitchen are good enough to handle the time limit.

"Now you can start to prepare your filling. Depending on the flavours you've chosen, you can use a buttercream, jam, or ganache to fill the centre. I'll be doing a vanilla buttercream that I'll be layering inside with fresh blueberries." It's one of my favourite combinations, and one that I feel really exhibits the exquisiteness of the macaron shells and the fruit inside. "This is where you're going to be incorporating your magic."

No one moves as I make up the basis of my buttercream, and it's impossible to shake the feeling of being watched, but I know I have to.

Once the mix is made, I pick up my wand and clear my throat. "You need ultimate focus when you infuse the magic. You should be pointing your wand at the middle of the mixture and send all of your thoughts into it. I'm going to focus on one of my favourites, *resilience*."

Antonio quirks an eyebrow, but doesn't say anything as I point my wand at the centre of the buttercream mixture. If I get this wrong, I can end up messing it up badly. Just like when Oakley managed to infuse her cupcakes with thunder instead of warm fuzzy love.

That almost ended very badly for her. And for the shop in general.

Magic zings through me, and a small shower of sparks make their way into the bowl, though admittedly that's mostly for show. Sometimes people find it hard to imagine magic going into something if they can't actually see it.

Satisfied, I set my wand down and give the buttercream a quick mix to make sure it goes all the way through.

I grab a clean spoon and dip it into the mixture to take a small sample. "It's really important that you taste anything you infuse with magic before it's put into the final product," I say. "If you don't, then you risk serving something that doesn't make your consumer feel the way they're supposed to, which is naturally not a good thing." I take a small bite of the buttercream, relieved to find myself feeling fortified by the resilience I put into it. Perhaps I should have eaten something like this before I started giving my class.

"May I taste too?" Antonio asks.

"Of course." I push the bowl over to him and watch intently as he takes a spoon of his own.

I'm not sure why it worries me so much to think of him trying it, especially when he would at the end of the class anyway.

"It's good," he says.

"Thanks."

The timer goes off, making me jump a little before I remember what it's there for.

"All right, everyone, it's time to take your macarons out of the oven now. You need to slide the baking parchment off the tray and leave them to cool for a few minutes. Once that's done, you can start peeling them off. You should only be adding the filling once they're completely cool, but I have some I made earlier for you all to try while we're waiting."

The noise of multiple ovens opening and closing

fills the room, and the air is filled with the sweet smell of meringue shells.

It smells like home, and for the first time since starting to teach my class, I start to relax and enjoy myself. I'm sure I have a lot of questions to answer, but I feel much more confident doing it now I've done the baking part.

I wonder how much of that is to do with the way Antonio has been supporting me through the demonstration. I didn't think I needed an assistant until now, but I'm definitely changing my mind, especially if I ever do this again.

THREE

ANTONIO

I ROLL my eyes and curse the students for leaving things all over the place. It's not the first time, and I'm not naive enough to think that it's the last.

"Do you want me to stay and help?" Hazel asks, making me jump.

I turn to face the gorgeous blue-haired witch. I'm not sure what it is about her that I find so enthralling, the big brown eyes, or the way she moves around a kitchen.

Probably both.

"No, I've got this," I say, turning my curses on

myself when I realise I could have spent more time with her if I'd said yes.

"If you're sure."

"You're a guest demonstrator, I know you're not paid enough to stay and clear up too."

She chuckles. "You're not wrong there. I hope they're paying the regular instructors better, we can't all do this for the love of cake."

I smile at her answer. She's not wrong. And in my case, I don't do anything for the love of cake. If I could avoid making another one for the rest of my life, then I'd be happy. Dad wouldn't be, but that might cease to matter at some point.

"Would you like these?" she asks, offering me a box of macarons.

"Can't you sell them at your bakery?"

She shakes her head. "They're not made in the right environment."

Ah, of course. They'll have their kitchen set up to avoid common allergens and other contaminants.

"Then yes, please. D-DeRossi will want to try some I'm sure." Oops, I nearly called him *Dad* in front of a fellow chef. I've worked as his sous for years and I still find it hard to remember to call him the right thing. It's a strange rule when everyone knows we're related anyway.

"Great, I'll just leave them here." She hesitates for

a moment, as if she wants to ask me something else, then clears her throat. "Anyway, thanks for having me. It's been fun."

I resist the urge to ask her if she means that, especially as she seemed quite nervous when she was actually doing her demonstration.

"Thank you for coming in, it was enlightening."

Her whole face lights up as she smiles. "I'm glad you thought so."

"I do." And I'd actually like to know more about the possibilities of imbibing magic into food. I wonder if it's only possible with stable things like baked goods, or if it could be incorporated into sauces and meats.

Perhaps it's something I need to learn more about.

"I'll see you around." She gives me a little wave and leaves the room.

I watch her leave, wishing I could have asked her the dozens of questions racing through my mind. Instead, I force myself to focus on putting everything back in the right place.

We need to teach the students to tidy as they go better or they're in for a rude awakening when they start working under an actual chef.

"Antonio?" Dad says.

"In here," I respond.

"Ah, good. I was looking for you," he responds in Italian.

"I'm just finishing tidying." I gesture to the pots that have been left on the side.

He raises an eyebrow. "Did our guest not clean up after herself?"

"She did," I say quickly, anxious to defend Hazel for some reason. "It's the students who are the messy ones."

"Mmm. How was she?"

Mesmerising, but it's probably best not to say that.

"She was a bit nervous," I admit. He'll probably learn as much from the students if he asks them anyway. "But nothing unexpected. They seemed to learn a lot from her."

"Good, good."

"She left some macarons if you want to try one of them." I gesture to the small box sitting on the worktop next to us.

Dad's eyebrows shoot up. He must be surprised that she thought to leave some behind, not everyone who comes in to give a guest demonstration thinks to.

He picks one up and sniffs it. To some people, it may look like he doesn't trust it, but I know that he's just trying to sense what flavours she decided to use. He bites into it with the satisfying crunch that only comes from a good macaron, and nods his approval.

"What emotion did she put into it?" he asks.

"Resilience."

He raises an eyebrow. "Interesting choice."

"What did you expect?" I try not to let my interest shine too much. I don't want him to start questioning what I want from my career, it'll just lead to another argument where he accuses me of not appreciating everything he's given me, or the skills he's taught me. And that's not quite an accurate reflection of how I feel.

"Something cuter."

A small smile pulls at my lips. "Me too. But I don't know enough about the market to know whether that's a good choice of emotion."

"Hmm." He takes another bite, clearly thinking while he chews. "Perhaps we should send someone down to the bakery to do some market research."

"I could go." The words are out of my mouth before I can think twice about it.

To my surprise, Dad just nods. "Yes, yes. You know what you're looking for and she's met you."

"I had a few more questions I wanted to ask after the demonstration, I could see if she'll answer those too?"

"Do as you will, just make sure you're here for the classes you need to assist at," he says.

"I will."

"I'm going to be away for a few days. The patisserie needs my presence apparently." His voice betrays how annoyed he is about the fact my cousin is messing it up. I know Dad wants to give him a chance to prove himself, but Geoffrey's skills as a patissier leave a lot to be desired.

"I'll make sure everything runs smoothly in your absence," I promise. Not that I need to. When we took on the cookery school a few years ago, it was already running like a well-oiled machine. I suspect we could disappear for months at a time and nothing would change about it. Which is reassuring for me, not so much for Dad.

"I know you will. And call your mother, she's nagging me."

"I called her last night."

"Good boy." He picks up another macaron and walks out of the room, leaving me to stew in my thoughts.

And to come up with what I'm going to say when I walk into the Broomstick Bakery and see Hazel again.

FOUR

Hazel

I HUM to myself as I mix a big batch of creme paté. It's a simple recipe that I've made dozens of times, and I don't need to concentrate too hard, especially when it's not being infused with magic. I'll be doing that part when I make up the actual patisseries.

The door creaks open and Rowen steps inside. "Did you see the order we got?" she asks.

I shake my head. "What's it for?"

"A croque-en-bouche."

I groan and look at the sky. "Why do you hate me?" I ask the non-existent pastry gods.

"You're the one who said we should put it on our

list of services," Rowen points out, ever the eldest sister. Technically, she isn't wrong. I am the one who suggested putting them on the menu.

"Because they look good. I never thought people would actually order them."

"Then you don't know people very well." She doesn't wait for me to reply and heads towards the back with a big sack of flour. In about half an hour, the whole kitchen is going to smell of cooking biscuits.

I'll never admit it to her, but I love that smell. It's like a treat for my nose. I think I may even prefer it to patisserie, though that definitely isn't true when it comes to making it. There's something magical about taking a bunch of simple ingredients and turning it into something intricate and beautiful.

Between the noise of the mixers and the extractor fans in the kitchen, it's impossible for me to make conversation with my sister, but I don't mind. We're used to working in the same room together without saying anything.

The door leading to the shop creaks open and Clover pokes her head around. "We're running low on the blackberry and apple tarts, do you have more?"

I shake my head. "I can make some up, but we've only got enough blackberries for one more batch."

"That should see us through until tomorrow. I can go to the market and get you more than."

"Thanks." I smile at my sister, grateful for her help. This is one of the best bits about working in a business with the three of them. We can help one another when we need to. And it makes sense that Clover's going to help me with this, the apple and blackberry tarts have been flying off the shelves ever since one of the locals posted on social media about them.

I take my creme paté over to the fridge to rest and start collecting the ingredients for the pastry, glad this one is shortcrust and not puff. It only takes me a couple of minutes to start the dough going, and I quickly get into the rhythm of making the tarts. I've baked them so many times that I don't need to think too hard about the method and I just let my hands do the baking.

It isn't until I have the apple and blackberry compote stewing on the stove that I pull out my wand. I take a deep breath and focus all of my attention on the feeling of warmth. I want the people who eat these tarts to feel as if they're experiencing a warm hug.

Magic tingles through my entire body and sparks erupt from the end of my wand, scattering amongst the apple in the same way the cinnamon I've already added did. Sometimes, I think it might be easier if we imbibe the spices in advance, but then I remember the time we tried it and Rowen's gingerbread men ended up feeling loud and confusing.

At least they were still tasty.

With the compote cooling and the slices of apple for the top sliced and lightly caramelised, I start clearing down my workspace. There's nothing worse than mess everywhere.

The door to the shop opens again and Clover steps inside.

"I'm nearly done," I say without waiting for her to prompt me. "Everything is just resting."

"Oh, I'm not here about the tarts." A wide grin spreads across her face.

"You're not?" I frown.

"Nope. Do you want to tell me why there's a sexy Italian guy in the shop asking for you?"

"There is?" I'm even more surprised than she is. "Are you sure he's here to see me?"

"Do you know anyone else called Hazel Parkes?"

"Actually, I do. There was this girl…"

"Hazel," she cuts me off sharply. "That's not the point. He's here to see you."

"Did he give you a name?" Because I doubt it's

sexy Italian guy. Though now I think about it, I do know one attractive Italian.

"Antonio De…something. I didn't catch the rest of it."

"Antonio's here?" My heart skips a beat at the idea of DeRossi's sous chef coming to visit me. Did I leave something behind after my demonstration the other day?

"Are you dating someone we don't know about?" Clover asks.

"No, no. He's here about my class the other day."

"Interesting. So there's no problem if I ask him on a date?"

"Clover!"

"All right, all right. He's all yours. But you shouldn't keep him waiting too long. Why don't you take him down to Cauldron Coffee Shop? Willow asked us to deliver a batch of shortbread anyway and I haven't had time."

I nod. That doesn't sound too bad. "Okay, tell him I'm coming in a moment, I just need to wash my hands and hang up my apron." And run a comb through my hair. I always hate how tangled it gets when it's been up in a hair net all day.

"I'm not sure he's going to wait that long."

"He's a sous chef, he'll understand." And if he doesn't, then that's his problem and not mine.

Clover disappears back into the shop, hopefully to tell him I'll be right out. I give my table one last wipe down and then run upstairs to tidy myself up. I'm not sure why it bothers me how presentable I am to Antonio when we've only met once, but I want to make a good second impression on him, especially if he's here on behalf of his boss.

FIVE

ANTONIO

HAZEL PUSHES open the door to a coffee shop and steps inside. I follow behind, wondering what the connection between Broomstick Bakery and the coffee shop is.

"Hey, Willow." Hazel waves at the dark-haired woman behind the counter. "I brought the shortbread you ordered." She heads straight to the counter and puts down the box she's been carrying since we left Broomstick Bakery. I follow behind, unsure what I'm supposed to be doing.

"Thanks, Hazel. Azíl, will you put them out?" she asks the man behind the counter.

He nods and takes the box from her.

"They've been selling like hotcakes. Which doesn't surprise me. They go perfectly with a nice pumpkin spice latte," Willow says.

"Oh, I can see how. Though it's a little out of season for that, isn't it?" Hazel responds.

Willow chuckles. "It's not going to stop you ordering one though, is it?"

"Absolutely not. Antonio, what would you like?" she asks, turning to me with a curious expression on her face.

"Just a black coffee, please."

"Coming right up." The barista disappears behind the counter to start making our drinks. "You should have a seat."

Hazel leads me to a comfortable set of chairs and sits down, smiling reassuringly at me.

"People normally argue with me more about what kind of coffee I want," I say offhandedly.

"That must be annoying," Hazel responds. "But Willow's not like that. She takes too much pride in the quality of her coffee to need to pressure anyone into ordering anything fancier."

"You seem to know her well."

"She's my cousin."

Ah, that explains something. Apparently, I'm not the only one who works with my family members.

"Here you go, on the house," Willow says, setting down two good-sized mugs on the table between us, each of them branded with a black and orange logo.

"Thank you," I say.

"Anything for a friend of Hazel's." She disappears back behind the counter.

I shift uncomfortably in my seat.

"Don't worry, she's not flirting," Hazel assures me. "Azíl's her...something."

"Something?" I raise an eyebrow.

"What would you call a three thousand-year-old cursed warlock that came out of a teapot?"

I frown. "I have a lot of questions."

"And now you know why he's her *something*. One day she's going to have to tell me the whole story, but the basics seem to be that Azíl was cursed to live in a teapot for a few thousand years, Willow's best friend found it and sent it here, then Willow accidentally released him and caused all kinds of problems, ending with the two of them living and working here together." She shrugs as if it isn't a big deal.

And maybe it isn't. I've personally never met any warlocks cursed to live inside kitchen objects, but maybe that's just good luck.

"Anyway, enough about Willow. What did you want to talk to me about?" Hazel asks.

I clear my throat, suddenly feeling more than a little nervous about what I have to ask. There's a good chance that what she demonstrated the other day was as much as she wants to tell people about her family secret. "I wanted to ask if you'd teach me more about what you do."

"Patisserie? I'd have thought you'd learn more as Chef DeRossi's sous than from me." She picks up her mug and blows across the top.

"About classic patisserie, maybe. But not about this specific part of it."

"You mean the magic." She takes a sip and studies me intently.

"The magic," I confirm.

"I'm not sure you'll find it particularly interesting, but if you want to, then sure. On one condition?"

"Name it."

Her eyebrows shoot up. "You don't know what I'm going to ask yet. What if I tell you that my condition is that you have dinner with my older sister?"

"Then I'd do it, but I'd rather have dinner with you." The words slip out before I have a chance to think about them.

A small blush crosses her cheeks, but she clears her throat. "Luckily for you, I have no such demands.

But if you want me to teach you one of my patisserie secrets, then you have to teach me one of yours."

"I don't have any patisserie secrets."

"You're Chef DeRossi's sous chef." The way she says his name almost sounds as if he's some kind of idol to her. Maybe he is, but that's a strange thing to think about when he's just my dad.

"I am," I say carefully, unsure where she's going with this.

"Which means you've got to be an incredibly talented chef in your own right. You must have secrets." She sits back in her seat with an adorable satisfied grin on her face.

I sit in silence, unable to fully process what she's saying. She thinks that I'm Dad's sous chef because I'm talented, not just because I'm his son. Maybe she's trying to butter me up for something, but I don't think she's that kind of person.

Which means she believes it. She thinks *I'm* a good chef.

"Okay. I'll swap one of your secrets, for one of mine," I suggest.

"Excellent."

"You're not going to specify what you want me to teach you?" I ask.

"No. You know your skills far better than I do. I'd

rather you just surprised me." She takes another sip of her coffee, reminding me that my own is there.

I pick up the mug and discover the most delightful smell coming from it. I can see why Hazel's cousin is proud of her coffee.

"What if I teach you something you don't find useful?"

"Everything is useful if you know the best way to apply it." She pushes a strand of blue hair behind her ear.

Is it some kind of spell she uses to change the colour? I can think of a couple that would do the trick.

"Do you use much magic when you're cooking?" she asks, revealing that she's already worked out I'm a warlock even if I haven't told her.

Of course, if she looks up to Dad the way she seems to, she'll already be aware that he is, and therefore I am.

"Not very often. I know some chefs like to use it to make things quicker, but it doesn't feel like I have the same kind of control if I do that."

She nods along, seeming to understand, which makes sense. She barely used any magic other than the colouring of her macarons and imbibing the emotion in the first place.

"I know what you mean. I learned the hard way

the first few times I tried to use magic to make Italian meringue."

"Let's guess, you over whipped the eggs?" It's what I did when I tried. Dad just stood by and watched, knowing it would teach me a valuable lesson.

"I wish it was as simple of a mistake as that. I tried to use magic to pour the sugar in and ended up burning myself and almost destroying Granny's worktop." A warm smile spreads over her face, as if she's recalling a pleasant memory.

"Is she the one who taught you to cook?"

"She taught me to bake, yes. Actually, it was in the bakery kitchens on a Saturday afternoon. She used to shut up the shop and she'd take us down there and teach us all of her tricks."

"Us?"

"My sisters and I. My brother was too young at the time. But the five of us would be in that kitchen every week. In spirit, I suppose we still are, though Granny rarely comes by now she's handed over the reins to us."

"Ah, so the woman behind the counter..."

"Was one of my sisters, yes. Clover, she makes the most delicious baklava you've ever tasted in all kinds of variations."

"Maybe I'll have to try some."

"Oh, you will. If you come by the shop tomorrow after we close for a lesson in magic imbibing, she'll probably be there experimenting. She likes to do it at night."

"That would be good." I take a sip of my coffee. "You specified that your grandmother taught you baking, but not your patisserie?"

A small smile lifts the corners of her lips. "Good catch, you're paying attention."

"Any decent chef needs to."

She lets out a light laugh, a delightful sound that I hope to hear more of. "True. But you're right. Granny is more of a rustic and traditional baker, but I wanted something more than that. That's when I started taking courses and enrolled in a culinary school. It was there that I really fell in love with patisserie. What about you? How did you come to be a chef?"

"Nepotism," I mutter.

Hazel chuckles. "Hey, no shame there. That's how I got into it too. It doesn't make a difference if your passion is there for it."

"That's a nice way to look at it." I need to plan something impressive to show her tomorrow so I can prove her right. I want her to know that I'm as passionate about food as she is, even if it's not necessarily in the same way. While Dad wants me to be the pastry chef who follows in his footsteps, that's not what I want in my heart.

Maybe Hazel is the person who I can finally share that with.

"So, other than nepotism, how did you get into it?"

"Dad used to get me to help make dinner every Wednesday night, and Mama used to always make me help with the pasta. When I was old enough, Dad got me a job in the kitchen he was working at, and from there, I worked my way up to being a sous chef."

"It must have been a prestigious kitchen for there to be a position for a pastry sous."

"It was."

She sighs wistfully.

"Is it something you want to do?" I ask. "Work in a kitchen instead of your own bakery?" I drain the rest of my coffee, impressed by the flavour. I'll have to see if I can get some of the beans for Mama.

"Not really. Sometimes I wonder about having a different job, but I like the fact that I can create and invent. The shop gives me the freedom to do that, and to go where the ingredients take me."

The way she talks about it makes it clear to me that she has an intense passion for the food she's creating. It makes me like her even more.

She sighs and finishes her own coffee. "But speaking of pastries, I need to get back so I can finish my apple and blackberry tarts."

"I'm sorry, I didn't mean to keep you so long."

"Don't be, I've enjoyed talking to you, Antonio."

Hearing my name come from her like that sends a shiver through me. There's something about her that's captivating my attention more than anyone else ever has.

"I look forward to our lesson tomorrow," I say.

"Me too." She gets to her feet and grabs both of our mugs, taking them back over to the counter and saying goodbye to her cousin.

Dad found someone really special when he extended an invitation to speak to Hazel.

And I don't think it's all about her cakes.

SIX

Hazel

A SMALL PART of me wonders if it was a good idea to say yes to teaching Antonio more about imbibing magic into patisserie, but all of my worries flee the moment the bell above the door of the shop rings, announcing his arrival.

Clover throws me an amused glance from where she's finishing soaking a tray of fresh baklava in syrup. "Ah, has your handsome Italian arrived?"

"He's not my Italian," I mutter.

"But he is handsome?" She raises an eyebrow.

"I have eyes. And ears." The sound of his voice matches the rest of him with his warmth and attractiveness. I don't think anyone can deny that Antonio is a handsome man.

"Mmhmm."

"Are you going to be here all night?" I ask.

"Give me ten minutes and then I'll leave you to your take-me-to-bed games."

"What? That's not what we're doing. We're just going to do some baking."

"Say whatever you want, Zel, I know you, and I know how you act when you like a guy." The way she says it is so matter of fact.

"Shows what you know. Now I'm going to greet my guest, and then we'll do some very *innocent* baking." I give my hands a quick wash.

"The more you protest, the less I believe you," Clover mutters as I step out of the kitchen.

Antonio's face lights up as he sees me. "Hello."

"Hey. Let me just lock up and then we can go back to the kitchens," I say, slipping out from behind the counter so I can lock the front door.

If Antonio visits again, I'll tell him to use the side one so we don't have to leave this one open.

"Come on back. Clover's just finishing up, but then we'll have the kitchen to ourselves," I say.

"Great." He follows me into the kitchen.

A small clatter from the back reveals where

Clover has gotten up to. She must be putting away her tray of baklava to soak overnight.

I turn in time to catch his expression and the surprise flitting across his face. "Not what you were expecting?" I ask.

He chuckles. "That obvious?"

"Your face said it all."

"From what you described, I thought it was going to be more like a farmhouse kitchen, not..." He waves his hand around the room.

Satisfaction wells up within me. "We renovated a few years ago. Before that it looked a bit more like you'd expect."

"I know a lot of chefs who would be jealous of your setup."

"Thank you."

"That's me done for the night," my sister says as she comes back into the room. "Hi, I'm Clover, we didn't get to properly meet before." She holds out her hand.

"Antonio." He shakes her hand, but doesn't linger nearly as long as he did when he greeted me.

Which shouldn't matter.

"I'll see you in the morning, Hazel," she says, throwing me a meaningful look as she leaves through the side door.

Antonio frowns. "Does she not live here?"

I shake my head. "Only my eldest sister lives here."

"Ah, interesting. So, what's first?" he asks, looking around for any clues that I might have left hanging around.

"I thought we'd start with tasting." I lead him to a small booth in the back of the kitchen. It's normally where we do taste testing of any new products one of us wants to try.

It's only once we're sat down that I realise how close together we're now sitting, especially with where I put the plates. I hope he doesn't think that I'm being oddly forward or something.

"Do you prefer still or sparkling water?" I ask.

"Still."

"I'm glad you said that, sparkling would have meant going to the fridge." I pick up the jug I put on the table earlier and fill up both of our glasses. "I wasn't sure what you wanted to learn about this most, so I thought this would be a fun way to do flavour and emotion at the same time. But if you want to do something more hands-on, that's okay, I can get some ingredients out."

"No, this is good," he says. "I'm not actually sure what I want to learn in particular. After your demonstration, I was just left with the feeling that I wanted to know more."

"It's a good job I didn't put curiosity into the macarons then," I joke.

"Can you do that?"

I nod. "I think it would work with just about any emotion so long as the witch or warlock casting the spell knows it well enough. But there are plenty I've never tried."

"Like what?"

"Most of the negative emotions, though I've tasted those put into things by accident."

"That sounds like a disaster waiting to happen."

"Oh yes. When you meet Oakley, you should ask her about what happened at the wedding she made cupcakes for."

"That sounds like something she'd rather a strange man didn't bring up with her," he observes.

"Fair point."

"What other emotions haven't you tried?"

"Well I've never tried seduction or anything along those lines." A fierce blush rises to my cheeks, but I'm not sure why. I don't normally get flustered when talking about these things.

Then again, I'm not normally sat quite so close to attractive Italian chefs with intense gazes either.

"Why not? I'd have thought they'd be good sellers around Valentine's day."

"We talked about it, but we felt that was crossing

the line into dangerous territory as far as consent is concerned."

"Ah, that makes sense. Good call."

"But I think it could be different in a restaurant setting," I say quickly.

"What makes you say that?"

"Well, if a couple are in a restaurant and they want to order a seduction and strawberry cheesecake or something like that, then they both know they're doing it, so they're both consenting to the results of it. But if someone comes in and buys a pair of seductive strawberry tarts, then we don't know if she's going to tell the other person what she's giving them."

"Ah, I see." A contemplative expression crosses his face. "Isn't that the same with the rest of the emotions too?"

"Honestly, yes, I think it could be. And that's why I think you should need a licence to sell these kinds of things. But we decided on the whole that by making it clear what each of our products is, and choosing our emotions carefully, we're doing everything we can. There's a lot less damage that can be done by giving someone a cupcake that'll make them feel warm and fuzzy, versus a chocolate that will make them want to jump someone's bones."

He chuckles. "That's quite an image you conjure up there."

"I'm only assuming that's what seduction feels like to eat." I shrug. "I've never actually tried it."

"Maybe someday you'll find someone you can safely try it with."

"Perhaps." I push a strand of hair behind my ear and look away to try and conceal my nervousness talking to him about these kinds of things.

And the thoughts of him being the one I'd try it with that are popping into my head.

I clear my throat. "Anyway, after all that talk of clearly labelling things, why don't you try this biscuit and tell me what you think is in it." I push one towards him.

He lets out an amused laugh. "I can sign a waiver if you want?"

"I think that's okay, I promise none of these should make you do anything weird."

"Good to know." He picks up the biscuit and takes a bite.

I watch him intently, trying to ignore how dry my mouth has become. I don't normally react this way around people.

"That's good," he says, setting down the half-eaten biscuit. He's probably noticed the volume of other things on the table and doesn't want to fill himself up too much. "I feel very festive."

"You should, that's a festive cheer gingerbread, one of our specialities around the holidays. I had Rowen make a batch earlier."

"You didn't make this one?"

I shake my head. "Rowen is the one with the talent for biscuits."

"Ah, so which did you make?"

I pull a plate with an apple and blackberry tart towards him, suddenly self-conscious about if it's good enough. The man next to me is Chef DeRossi's sous chef, he's going to have seen some of the best pastry work in the world.

And now he's going to be judging mine.

"I normally do the patisserie," I explain. "Clover works on the baklava and things like palmiers, while Oakley does the cupcakes and any birthday cakes we have on order." I point to each example of my sisters' craft, feeling pride for how good they are well up inside me.

"What about your brother?" Antonio asks.

I hide my surprise that he's remembered I have one, most people forget. "Ash is at Grimalkin Academy still, he's in his third year."

"Ah, so not part of the family business."

"He runs some errands for us sometimes." From

things he's said, I suspect my youngest sibling does want to join the bakery staff, but he hasn't plucked up the courage to actually tell us yet.

Antonio goes straight for my tart.

I bite my bottom lip, trying not to let my nerves overwhelm me. What if he doesn't like it?

Worse, what if he tells Chef DeRossi I'm a bad baker?

I push the thoughts out of my head. Antonio is too nice to say any of that, and he's definitely not going to do it to my face.

"This is delicious," he says. "You've got just the right amount of cinnamon in it."

"Thank you."

"And it makes me feel warm, but in a different way to how the festive gingerbread made me feel."

I nod. "Festive wouldn't feel quite right with this one. If you're around in November, you should come and try my Bonfire Night toffee apple tart, that one's always a hit."

"What do you put in that one?"

"It's hard to explain, but it's like the warmth of the fire, the excitement of the fireworks, and the crispness of the air. Do you know the feeling?"

He nods. "I've only been to one Bonfire Night, but I know what you mean."

"Oh, right. You don't celebrate it in Italy."

"It would be weird to celebrate the night the UK's parliament building didn't blow up there, yes."

"It's weird to celebrate it here too," I point out.

"Maybe." He pulls one of Oakley's cupcakes towards him and sweeps a finger along the frosting, putting it in his mouth.

My breathing hitches, but I don't think he notices, which is probably for the best. The last thing I need is for him to realise how much he's affecting me and to start thinking that I'm not professional.

"Oh, that makes me feel fluffy."

I chuckle. "That's a favourite at weddings. It's supposed to be newlywed joy."

"I can feel it. And the frosting texture is divine."

"She's really good at it," I agree. Nobody makes cupcakes like Oakley.

We go through each of the other cakes and pastries on the table, with him guessing the emotions and the flavours of each with surprising ease. His palette is something else.

Even if we don't cook anything tonight, it's been a lot of fun. And maybe it's for the best if we don't.

That just means I get to see him again.

SEVEN

HAZEL

IT FEELS as if I've eaten a whole bowl of Oakley's newlywed bliss frosting. Not that I'd do that, it takes her a good amount of time and effort to make, and it would make me sick. But it's like the emotion has completely overtaken everything else.

Perhaps I need Rowen to make me a shortbread full of concentration.

Not that I normally go around eating our products to control my emotions.

As if my thoughts summon her, Rowen appears from upstairs, looking as impeccably turned out as normal with her curly dark hair somehow under control and in a neat bun. She always knows how to look the part of a business owner, and I never feel quite as serious when I'm next to her.

"Morning, Row."

"You're here early," she says, looking me up and down as if there's something out of place.

I smooth down my apron, "I'm here at my normal time when I need to make macarons," I point out, checking the clock just to make sure I'm right.

Yep. I'm on time. Doing my normal thing.

"You were here late last night, I thought you might be late to rise today."

"Oh, right, yes. But it was just a work thing."

She raises an eyebrow and heads to the coffee maker, pressing a couple of buttons to start her morning cup. She never drinks coffee upstairs any more, not since Willow gifted us one of her old machines when she upgraded.

"A work thing?"

"You sound like you don't believe me."

She puts a second mug under the spout of the machine, knowing I'll want one too, especially if she's planning on continuing to give me a talking to.

"How many work things do you know that last until eleven at night and involve special batches of gingerbread?" she asks.

"You said you were okay with that."

"Of course I am, we'll sell the rest of the gingerbread today, you know people ask us for it all year round."

"So what's the problem?"

Rowen sighs and hands me one of the coffees, gesturing towards the booth.

That's not a good sign. She only wants to go there when she's going to tell one of us off. Normally, it's not me in the firing line, but today seems to be different.

I sigh and slide into the booth, knowing there's no point putting this off. Rowen won't stop until she's had her say, even if that means hanging around the kitchen and bothering me while I'm trying to prep food.

"Lay it on me," I say once she's taken a seat.

A small smirk lifts the corners of her lips. "How do you know I'm going to say anything?"

"You get this look on your face when you're about to give one of us a lecture. It's like you forget that we have two perfectly good parents who can do it for you."

Rowen laughs. "I can call Mum on you if you prefer."

"I'd rather you didn't, especially when I'm not sure what you're planning on lecturing me about."

"No lecture, I promise. I just want to ask if you know what you're doing."

"What do you mean?"

"With Antonio."

"Oh, that. We didn't do anything, we just tasted examples of the things we make here and talked about them."

"So you didn't show him any of the family secret recipes?" Rowen asks.

My eyebrows jump up to my hairline. "Is that what this is about? You not wanting me to give out family secrets?"

"It's important we protect the things that make us money," Rowen says.

I resist the urge to laugh. "It's nothing to do with our family recipes. He wants to learn about putting magic into food, and we're not exactly the only ones who do that. Bakeries up and down the country do it."

"But not like we do."

"No, not like we do." As far as I know, Broomstick Bakery was the first in the UK to introduce labels with the emotions imbibed in the food on them, and the first to start diversifying them to the extent we have. It's taken us from a small bakery that the locals come to every so often, to the kind of place people travel from miles around to visit. It's been good for business, but it's not exactly unique.

"I don't disagree. But the fact we do it isn't a secret, that's why we're successful at it."

"Hmm."

"But no, I'm not passing on any family recipes or anything like that."

"Mmhmm."

It's impossible to stop the loud sigh escaping me. "What's wrong now?"

Rowen clears her throat. "You're protecting yourself, right?"

I narrow my eyes. "From what? I thought you were just interested in knowing whether I was giving away family secrets."

"I don't want you to get hurt."

"Why would you think I'm going to?"

"I looked this Antonio up on the cookery school website."

"And..." What's she getting at? It isn't like Rowen to be this tactful about anything, she's more the kind of person who just says what she's thinking and doesn't care about the consequences. Not that she does it in a nasty way, it always comes from a concerned place.

"He seems like your type, that's all."

"I have a type?" My question comes out as more

of a squeak than anything else. Surely I haven't dated enough to actually have a type? I've had boyfriends, but they've never lasted particularly long.

"The way you were looking at him last night suggested that you thought he was your type, certainly."

My mouth falls open. "Did you spy on me?"

Rowen lets out a good-natured laugh. "I'm an older sister, I'm allowed to spy on you."

"No, you're not."

"I'm kidding," she promises. "I heard a noise at ten and thought you'd already left, so I came down to check everything was okay and saw the two of you sitting here. It didn't look like it was just about the food."

"It was," I counter quickly.

"Mmhmm. Just be careful, Hazel, I don't want to see you get your heart broken." She gets to her feet and heads out into the main shop with her coffee still in hand.

I cup my hands around my mug and lean back in my seat. Is she right? Am I risking my heart?

I had a good time with Antonio last night, and I'm looking forward to spending more time with him when I can. And not just to talk about food and learn some of his tricks. There's something about him that draws me to him.

It's probably just common interests.

But if that's not a good basis for something more, then I don't know what is. I'm willing to risk my heart for something that could be real if it comes down to it. Whether that will be necessary remains to be seen.

EIGHT

HAZEL

THE KITCHEN IS a bit of a mess, but I don't care. While I don't use magic for cooking in case of mistakes, using it to clean up normally isn't too much of a problem.

"All right, everything's in the fridge setting, now you have to tell me one of your cooking secrets," I say to Antonio.

"I just need ingredients."

"The fridges are all yours." I gesture in the right direction.

"There's no need, I brought my own."

I raise an eyebrow. "Isn't that a strange thing to do?"

"You'll see why."

"I trust you." Even as the words are out of my mouth, I realise I believe them. I *do* trust him.

He picks up the bag he arrived with and starts unpacking. My surprise deepens as he starts placing savoury ingredients on the prep counter. What's he planning? We do some savoury pastries on Fridays, but normally we stick to sweet. We've tried more often than that, but the customers just don't seem to buy them.

"I tried to think of an exciting secret I could tell you, but I kept coming up with nothing," he admits. "But then I realised there's a secret about me I can share."

I cock my head to the side, intrigue mounting within me. "A personal secret?"

"Kind of. It's still related to cooking."

"Does it have anything to do with the fact you seem to have the makings of a gourmet meal laid out?"

A small smile tugs at his lips. "Maybe."

"All right. Then why don't I be your sous chef for a bit and you can tell me all about it." I pick up an onion. "How do you want it chopping?"

"Diced, please."

I pull out one of the vegetable chopping boards and place it on the counter. It doesn't see many onions, and mostly gets used for fruit, but that shouldn't be a problem.

With swift strokes, I make quick work of the onion and push the diced cubes into a bowl. "Okay, I have to ask what's going on. Why am I chopping an onion and not walnuts?"

Antonio sighs. "What's the most shameful thing a pastry chef could admit?"

"That they buy their puff pastry instead of making it," I quip.

He chuckles, a warm sound that fills me with emotions I can't fully describe. "All right, the second most shameful thing."

"Hmm. That they can't make a basic buttercream?"

"You're thinking too much like a patissier." The way his accent sounds around the word makes it so much more exciting than when I say it myself.

"Considering I am one, I'll take that as a compliment."

He picks up the onions and empties them into a skillet along with a healthy dose of butter. "I don't want to be a pastry chef."

My eyebrows raise. "Then why are you?"

He sighs. "Nepotism."

"I thought that was just how you became a chef?"

"It is, but it's also how I got into pastry in general. But this is what I've always wanted to do." He waves his hand at the sizzling pan.

"Cook onions?"

"No, just create dishes, menus, that kind of thing."

"Can't you do that as a pastry chef still?" I create things to put on our menu all the time. I know it isn't quite the same as working for a restaurant, but it still counts.

"I suppose so, but sometimes it doesn't feel like enough." He adds some garlic and herbs to the pan, shaking it. "How do you like your steak?"

"Rare."

"I'm glad you said that."

"What would you have done if I'd said medium?"

"Cooked you it medium," he responds. "I may personally think it's overdone, but it's your steak, not mine."

"If you don't want to be a pastry chef, why don't you try and get a job in a different department? You'd probably have head chefs falling over themselves to offer you a job." The way he's moving in the kitchen makes it clear that he knows exactly what he's done.

Antonio lets out a loud sigh but doesn't stop cooking. The kitchen is enveloped in the most delicious scent, and one that it doesn't normally witness.

I watch intently as he places two steaks into a new pan and turns his attention to the one I assume is going to make the rest of his sauce.

"Dad would never forgive me if I moved away from pastry," he admits.

"I'm sure that isn't true. He's your dad, he'll want you to be happy above and beyond."

"Would your grandmother have been happy if one of you hadn't wanted to be part of the bakery?" he asks as he adds cream to his pan.

"I believe so. But I see your point. It's hard to get rid of family pressure sometimes."

"Do you never wish that you weren't part of this business?"

I shake my head. "I love what I do."

"But do you love what you do *here*?"

A frown pulls at my forehead. "I enjoy working with my sisters, and having the freedom to create what I want so long as it's within the right parameters."

"But?"

"There isn't really a but," I admit. "There's some appeal to working in a professional kitchen, but I don't think I'd actually like it. I need too much creative freedom to be working within the expectations of another chef."

"You just said that you had to create within the right parameters," he points out.

"Yes, but they're parameters I set, that's different from having to do what a head chef wants. I'm sure you know that."

"I do." He pulls the steaks from the pan and allows them to rest while dealing with the rest of his sauce. "Do you have plates?"

I don't say a word as I grab them and some cutlery. I should have thought to warm them, but I was too focused on the conversation we were having.

He plates up quickly and we make our way over to the booth. My mouth waters at the sight of the plate he sets in front of me, and my stomach begins to rumble. I suppose this saves me from having to make something when I get home, though it isn't going to save me from Rowen's judgement in the morning.

I push that thought aside. My older sister isn't part of this situation, she doesn't get a say in it.

"This looks delicious," I tell him.

"Thank you. I know you won't find any emotions in it, but..."

"But?"

"I guess I was hoping that's what I could learn from you." He pauses. "How to put emotions into this kind of cooking rather than cakes and pastries. But now I've seen you working, I'm not sure it's going to be as easy as that, you seem to just enchant one part of it, and something that remains stable. A sauce wouldn't do that."

"Hmm. I don't know if the spell I use will work, but I'm sure there's something that would. A little adapting won't hurt anyone. We can try and figure it out, if you want?" The words are out of my mouth before I can stop them.

"I'd like that. But only if you actually like my cooking." He gestures to my plate.

I take a bite of my steak, making sure it's slathered in the delicious-looking sauce he's made. Even before I put it in my mouth. I chew slowly, enjoying the blend of different flavours.

"This is really good," I say, taking another bite almost straight away.

"I'm glad you think so."

"I definitely think we can do something to try and work out how to put magic in the sauce. It might take a few years, but it should be doable."

He beams at me. "You think so?"

I nod.

"And you're willing to work with me that long?" he asks.

"You're a brilliant chef with real talent, I'd be a fool not to," I return quickly.

"Thank you," he murmurs, seemingly not sure what to make of my compliment. "You have something on your cheek by the way." From the way he's said it, I think he's trying to change the subject.

"Oh, oops." I reach up and try to wipe it off.

He shakes his head, and taps a spot on his cheek.

I try again. "Gone?"

Antonio chuckles. "Somehow, you've made it worse. Do you have a napkin?"

I pull one out of the dispenser in the middle of the table and hold it out. He takes it from me and shuffles closer so he can wipe my cheek for me.

The world seems to still as I realise how close he now is. His knee brushes against mine and my breathing hitches.

What's wrong with me? I'm never like this around people.

Then again, Antonio isn't just anyone. There's something about him that just feels right. It's the way he talks about food, even if he isn't cooking the things he wants to be.

He brushes the napkin against my cheek and our

gazes lock. Neither of us move and the air feels with the promise of something I don't think I can name.

No. That's wrong. I can name it, I just don't want to for fear that I've got it wrong.

Antonio leans in and my eyes flutter closed, knowing what's coming next and welcoming it.

His lips brush against mine softly, filling my stomach with a torrent of butterflies.

To my surprise, instead of continuing the kiss, he leans back.

I open my eyes to find an alarmed expression on his face.

"I'm sorry, I don't know what I was thinking." His accent is stronger than normal, as if his worry over crossing a line he shouldn't have is making it come out more than before.

I reach out and touch his hand gently. "You were thinking that we were having a moment," I say.

His eyes snap up and meet mine again.

"But if you need me to say that it's okay if you kiss me, then consider this your permission." I bite my bottom lip, accidentally drawing his attention to it. Oops. I didn't mean that to come across the way it did.

On the other hand, the only thing I can think about now is kissing him properly, so if this furthers my cause, then so be it.

"Are you sure?"

I nod.

"How do you know I didn't put any seduction in your steak?"

I let out a small laugh. "Nice alliteration. But I know for three reasons." I hold up three fingers so I can count them off. "One, you said you didn't know how. Two, I watched you cook it."

"And three?"

"I trust you, Antonio. I know you wouldn't do that." The moment I say the words, I realise how true they are. I trust him. A lot more than I should given we only met a week ago.

But some things in life just slot right into place, and I feel like this is one of them.

"Then I'd like to kiss you."

"Good." I'm the one who moves closer this time. I reach out and put my hand on his cheek, letting my focus slip so I can enjoy the moment and not think too much about it.

My eyes close just as his lips press against mine.

His kiss is firmer now, more certain in it now that he's sure it'll be reciprocated.

I wrap my arms around his neck, pulling him closer and deepening the kiss. It's everything I want it to be and more.

We break apart, each of us still in a bit of a daze.

"I suppose now would be a good time to ask you on a date?" Antonio asks.

I chuckle. "It probably is." A small part of me wants to ask if this dinner counts as a date, but I'm not sure what the answer will be.

"Is that a yes?"

"Yes." A wide smile spreads over my face. This isn't what I thought the evening would go, but it's a nice surprise, and one I plan on making the most of.

NINE

ANTONIO

THE BAKERY BELL tinkles as I step inside. I'm pretty sure it's a good thing that Hazel has asked me to pick her up from her family shop, it means she's told her sisters that she's going on a date.

Or just that she's spending time with me.

"Hi, Antonio," Clover says brightly as I step inside.

"Hey." I give her a half-wave. "Do they always stick you behind the counter? You always seem to be the one in the front."

"It's just my turn," she says brightly. "Normally Oakley does this shift, but she's been getting a lot of wedding orders recently and they take up a lot of her time. I don't mind though, the bakery works because we all work together." She's full of energy as she moves around. I can see similarities to the way Hazel moves around the kitchen.

As if summoned by my thoughts, Hazel appears from the back of the shop. Her gaze lands on me and she instantly smiles. "Not a minute late," she says.

"I promised I wouldn't be," I respond.

"I'll be back later," she tells her sister. "But there's more tarts in fridge three if you need them and I'll keep an eye on my phone in case there's an emergency."

"Uh-uh, we're not going to call you for anything," Clover responds. "Enjoy your date."

Ah, so she's told her sisters what we're doing, that's interesting. And welcome. I like that she's comfortable enough to do that.

I hold the door open for her and let her step out ahead of me.

"So, what's the plan?" she asks, turning to face me.

Her long blue hair is in loose waves around her face, framing it in a beautiful way that I haven't really seen from her before. The dress isn't like anything she's worn around me either. It's knee-length and flares around her waist, making her both look classy and cute at the same time.

"I'm not actually sure," I admit. "I haven't been on any dates in a while."

"Me neither."

That's reassuring, though I don't say as much, I don't want her to think that it matters to me how many people she might have dated in the past.

"But when I was coming up with things to do, I realised I had no idea where it was best to eat around here, or if there's anything fun to do."

"Ah, right. You'll have dated mostly in Italy, right?"

I chuckle. "Are you fishing for my dating history?"

A small blush crosses her cheeks. "Not at all."

I hold out my arm so she can slip her arm through it. She does, resting her hand on my sleeve and leaning into me slightly.

"I've never actually dated in Italy. I moved to England when I was ten."

"Did your whole family come?"

I shake my head. "Just me and my parents. My grandparents still live in Italy. I visit them most summers when I can. But that doesn't leave much time for dating."

"I see. So where did you grow up?"

"London, mostly."

"Ah, so a small town in the country isn't really

your speed." Regret tinges her voice. Probably because she thinks I don't like the town she lives in, which is as far from the truth as possible.

"I like this one," I assure her. "I think it suits me better, even if I haven't had a chance to explore much of it yet."

"Oh." Her whole face lights up.

"You've had an idea?" I ask.

"You said you hadn't planned anything for our date yet, right?"

"Right." When she puts it like that, I can see that I've made a mistake. How is she supposed to think I'm serious about this if I haven't planned?

"It's a nice day, why don't we go around some of the local shops and pick up some fresh produce and have a picnic? I know that's food and you're probably fed up of that, but it'll be fun."

And it'll mean that I get to spend lots of time with her.

"It's a good idea."

"Excellent, then we're going to start with cheese." She pulls me down a street, seeming to have a destination in mind.

"Why cheese?" I'm more curious than anything, but it isn't the produce I'd have chosen to start with.

"Because then we'll know which fruit wine to get,

and what vegetables we need. Trust me, cheese is the place to start."

I let out a low chuckle. "I trust you."

"Good. Because we're here." She stops in front of a small shop with a black framed window. Even from out here, I can see dozens of different types of cheese behind the counter. "This is what I love about being in a small town, everything is on my doorstep when I need it to be."

I only smile in response, but I don't think she was really talking to me anyway.

The moment I step inside the shop, I can smell the quality of the produce.

And Hazel seems to find it almost as exciting as I do. I can tell from the way she's leaning over the counter and chatting to the woman behind it.

I watch her intently, hardly believing that I'm on a date with someone who sees ingredients and food the way I do. I always assumed there'd be a mismatch between my work life and my home life, but maybe there doesn't have to be with someone like Hazel.

"What do you think?" she asks.

"Hmm?"

"Ah, so you weren't paying attention," she says triumphantly.

I chuckle. "You caught me." Perhaps I shouldn't be

watching her and thinking about how perfect she is. "What were you saying?"

"I was asking what you thought about blue cheese. I know some people hate it."

"I like it," I assure her. "You should pick, you know what's good."

"Oh no, I'm not falling for that. Come help." She gestures to the counter.

I step closer and lean over the counter, as close to Hazel as I can be without touching her.

Except, why am I not?

Tentatively, I reach out and place my hand on the small of her back. She leans into my touch, reassuring me that I'm doing the right thing and not going too fast.

As she points out the pros and cons of each cheese, I'm struck by the realisation that this doesn't feel like a first date. It feels like we've been doing this for years and that it's just part of our lives.

It feels right.

I just hope I'm not the only one who thinks that.

TEN

Hazel

"Does the name DeRossi mean anything to you?" Oakley asks, looking up from the pile of post she's sorting through.

"Yes. Why?"

"There's a letter addressed to Miss Parkes, but it doesn't specify which of us it's for," she responds, holding it out. "I'm guessing someone who forgot we're all Miss Parkes."

"Only until you get married," I say, taking it from her.

Oakley flushes. "That's not going to be any time soon."

"Uh-huh. I *totally* believe you."

"It's not. I'm not even engaged."

"You met Justin *at* a wedding," I point out. "And he knows that you're all romantic and gooey about these things. Mark my words, you'll be engaged before the end of the year."

"And what about you?" she returns with a sly grin.

"Hmm, what about me?"

Oakley raises an eyebrow. "Don't play coy with me. Rowen said you were all but jumping on the guy from the cookery school when he was here, and Clover said you looked like you were walking on air when you got back from your date yesterday."

I sigh and sit down opposite her. "It was amazing."

"Huh, that was easier to get from you than I expected."

I shrug. "He picked me up at the shop yesterday, it's not like I'm hiding what's going on."

"That's fair. So, when do I get to meet the future Mr Hazel Parkes?"

I snort. "He wouldn't be Parkes."

"Oh, then what would he be?"

A small frown mars my forehead as I realise that I've never asked Antonio what his surname is. "You know, I have no idea."

Oakley shakes her head, but I can tell from the smile on her face that she's more bemused than anything else. "Well, I can't wait. I've never seen you bouncing around the shop like this."

"Are you saying I'm never happy?"

"Not at all. You're easily one of the happiest people I know," she says.

I raise an eyebrow. I'm not sure how she can say that when she looks at herself in the mirror every morning. I swear Oakley was born with sunshine inside her, and everyone who meets her knows it.

"But there's still something different about you in the past week," she continues, not interrupted by my thoughts the same way I am. "I assume it's something to do with this chef."

"He's great," I admit. "We picked up a load of different food yesterday and spent hours in the park trying it all."

"Did he kiss you?" Oakley asks.

I glance away.

"Oh, he did."

"It erm, wasn't the first time," I admit. "He cooked for me after we talked about some of the theory of our baking the other day, and we kind of kissed then."

"You're blushing."

"I am not." I reach up and touch my cheek, surprised to find it a little warm. She may be right.

But I don't care.

"He sounds almost too perfect to be true," Oakley jokes.

"Didn't you think that about Justin too?"

She chuckles. "Yes, and then I learned that he likes to sleep with his socks on."

"Even after..."

"Mmhmm. He says feet weird him out."

"Does he make you wear socks too?" I'm not sure why that part makes a difference, but I think it does.

"No, but I bought some cute ones I'm going to wear next time he comes over anyway."

She's so in love it's almost sickening. But it makes sense to me that she's the one who fell first. Oakley's always been the romantic of the four of us.

"Anyway, what's your letter?" she asks, nodding to it.

"It's probably just an invoice for my payment for the demonstration." I rip it open and pull it out just to be sure.

I scan the piece of paper, not too sure if I'm reading it correctly.

"What is it?" Oakley asks. "I can see from your face that it's not what you think it is."

"Chef DeRossi wants to see me." My eyes widen and I stare at my sister, hardly able to believe the words that are coming out of my mouth.

"Why is that surprising? Isn't he the one who invited you to do the demonstration in the first place?" she asks.

"Yes."

"So he already asked to see you once, it shouldn't be too surprising that he's asking to see you again. Unless you think this has something to do with the fact you're dating his sous chef."

"I'm dating his sous chef," I repeat, leaning back in my seat and trying to process the information. "*How* am I dating Chef DeRossi's sous chef?"

"Let's see, you met, you got to know each other a bit, you cooked, you kissed, you said yes when he asked you out on a date..."

"Yes, yes, I know the logistics. It's more of a hypothetical how."

"I'm not sure I'm following."

"It's just that it's Chef DeRossi."

"Still not following," Oakley responds.

"He's an amazing chef, his desserts are inspirational and he's a genius..."

"Are you sure it's Antonio you want to date and not DeRossi?" she teases.

I roll my eyes. "Yes. I don't fancy Chef DeRossi."

"Ah, he's your professional crush. The person you want to be when you grow up." The expression on her face reveals she's completely understood how I feel, reassuring me that I'm not going completely crazy.

"I wonder what he wants?"

"Probably just to talk about your class with you," Oakley assures me. "Did he say anything about it when you left?"

I shake my head. "I didn't see him before I left. Though I did leave some macarons with Antonio for him. So maybe you're right."

"Hmm. Mysterious. I can't wait to find out what he wants."

"I'm sure we'll find out soon enough, he's asked me to come tomorrow."

"Oh good, there won't be much waiting around then." She gets to her feet. "I need to get a start on my cupcakes or I'll be late delivering. But I want to know everything that happens." She nods at my hand.

I glance down at the letter. What could Chef DeRossi possibly have to say to me? I'm nothing more than a pastry baking witch. Sure, my family has come up with a trick or two when it comes to magic and making our food that little bit extra special.

I let out a loud sigh. I suppose it doesn't matter too much, I'll only have to wait until tomorrow in order to find out what this is all about, and it's probably nothing I need to worry over. Not that it'll stop me doing just that.

ELEVEN

Hazel

I smooth my hands down the length of my skirt, ironing out nonexistent wrinkles. I'm not normally the nervous type when it comes to meetings, but that's because I'm the one who usually knows more.

But in this case, I'm meeting with Chef DeRossi. The man I've looked up to for almost a decade and who has shaped me into the patissier I am today, even if he has absolutely no reason to know that.

"Miss Parkes, it's good to see you again, why don't you come inside," Chef DeRossi says, gesturing towards his office door. His accent is a little more pronounced than Antonio's is, but I can hear some of the same notes in it. I wonder if they're from the same part of Italy.

"Thank you for taking the time to meet with me," I say.

A wry smile stretches over his face. "I think it should be me thanking you, Miss Parkes. I didn't give you very much notice."

Ah. Right. "It's okay, my sisters have got everything at the bakery covered." Partly because they're all too intrigued about what this could possibly be about. And because I normally spend most of the day in the back anyway. The patisserie doesn't last as long as the things the others make, which is both frustrating and liberating. I'm not sure I'd be able to spend an entire day talking to customers.

DeRossi nods.

"Was something wrong with the demonstration?" I've played back the events as many times as I can think of and not come up with anything that could be construed as bad. I was a bit nervous, but I think that goes with the territory to some extent.

"Not at all. But if you'd like to see some of the student feedback, I can email it to you. I think you'll be very pleased with it."

"Thank you, I'd like that." Not that I'll likely be giving a class or demonstration like that again, but it'll still be helpful information to know in case I ever do.

He makes a small note and then clears his throat. "I'm sure you're wondering what this is about."

"I am," I agree.

"I was wondering if you'd ever thought about teaching?" He presses his fingertips together as he waits for my response.

"Teaching?" My mind races as I try to put the pieces together and what this is going to mean, both for me, and for the bakery.

"Yes. We have an opening that I thought might interest you." He pulls out a sheet of paper and pushes it across the desk. "We haven't placed an advertisement for it yet. As I'm sure you can understand, I'd much rather bring someone onto the team whose pastry skills can be vouched for by a member of my team."

"Your team?" I'm not thinking straight, and I can tell from the way I'm reacting.

He nods. "You've been having one-on-one classes with my son, he's spoken very highly of your skills as a patissier, and of your teaching methods."

"Your son?" I don't think I've met his son, and even if I have, the only person I've been teaching anything to is Antonio.

Oh.

Oh.

"Antonio is your son?" I ask, wanting to be absolutely sure that I'm right before I start freaking out too much.

"He is, yes."

Everything slots into place. The things Antonio has said about his family and his father, the fact they have the same accent and even look similar. Somehow it completely slipped my notice that the two of them are related.

And Antonio never mentioned it. Did he really not think it was an important thing to talk about? We've even had conversations about his father, and now I'm learning he's the man opposite me.

I take a deep breath and force the thoughts out of my mind. I can deal with the Antonio problem later. Right now, I need to focus on the conversation I'm having with the older DeRossi.

"I assume there isn't going to be a problem with me continuing to work at Broomstick Bakery if I take the job?" I ask, picking up the sheet of paper he's given me. If there's a problem, then I'm going to have to say no right away.

From the expression on his face, that's something he's well aware of.

"I see it as an advantage that you do. Every day

we cook, we learn. And every time we learn, we become better teachers," he responds.

I nod, understanding what he means. I always feel like I improve my baking skills when I spend time making something new.

"When do you need me to decide by?" I ask, barely holding on to my shock and nerves over the revelation that the man I'm dating, and the idol I've had for years are related.

Am I only getting this job offer because I'm dating Antonio? A horrible feeling twists at my stomach as I consider the answer to that question. I don't want it to be true, but I fear it is.

"The end of the month," DeRossi responds. "And if you have any questions about it, please feel free to ask."

"Thank you. I'll think about it." I get to my feet and pause. "Thank you for the opportunity. This is something I never dreamed of."

He smiles somewhat dotingly at me, only fuelling my worry that I'm getting this offer because of my personal life and not my professional qualifications.

"I look forward to hearing your answer, Miss Parkes."

I smile tightly and nod, leaving the room with the job offer clenched tightly in my hand.

Somehow, getting the job offer of my dreams is turning into a nightmare. The paper burns my hand.

How could Antonio not tell me who his father is? Or about the job offer. I can't squash the idea that I've only had this conversation because of our dates. Does he even think I'm a good patissier, or is it all just a ploy to get me to date him?

Except that I wasn't lying when I told Anotonio that I trust him. How can that be true if I don't think there's some kind of explanation for this that doesn't involve deception?

I take a deep breath. I'm not ready to talk to him about it right now, but I'm going to have to. I feel like something very real has been growing between us, and I don't want to risk that by being difficult.

Nor do I want to waste an opportunity I've been dreaming of my entire professional career for this either.

My heart says to trust Antonio, and my head says he might have lied to me. And I'm not sure which of them to listen to.

TWELVE

Antonio

Dad walks in with a concerned expression on his face.

"What's up?" I ask in English.

He sighs. "I asked that witch you've been taking lessons with to come in for a chat."

I freeze. Does he know we've been dating? I haven't been hiding it, but I don't want him to think I have. "Hazel?"

"Yes. You spoke so highly of your one-on-one lessons, I thought it might be worth asking her if she'd take the patisserie class we need someone new for," he says.

"Oh." She'd be good at that, but I'm not sure whether or not she'll take it. "What did she say?"

"That she'd think about it, which is to be expected. I didn't think she'd be able to take it without some time."

I resist the urge to check my phone and see if she's messaged me. I know we haven't been seeing each other long, but it feels a lot more serious than just a fling. I hope she wants to talk to me about these kinds of things.

"She did seem surprised to learn that you're my son," Dad says. "Are you hiding me?"

"What? No, of course not," I say quickly. "I've no idea why she'd be surprised by that." We've talked about Dad a few times.

"Hmm. Are you sure she knew?"

I frown, thinking back over the conversations we've shared. "I just assumed she did."

"Perhaps you should make sure to tell her, that way it won't compromise the chances of her taking the job. She'd be an asset to the team."

"The job?" I demand. "You're thinking about the job right now?"

The confused expression on Dad's face is the only reminder I need that he's not completely up to date on the situation. "What else is there to think about?"

I start to pace, panic filling me at the idea of Hazel thinking I lied to her about this. Through omission, admittedly, and only by accident, but smaller things have broken budding relationships.

"Antonio?" Dad prompts when I don't say anything. He's probably worked it out. He's a smart man.

"We've started dating," I admit.

"That's something that would have been good to know *before* I offered her a job," Dad says.

"I didn't know you were going to offer it to her. I barely knew there was a job opening, you didn't include me in the decision," I snap. "And I thought she knew. Everyone knows."

"All right, calm down," he chides.

"How can I calm down? She thinks I lied to her," I point out.

"You don't know that." Dad steps forward and reaches out, placing a firm hand on each shoulder. "Take a deep breath, son."

I do as he commands, relieved to have someone else in control.

"You thought she knew who you were?" he asks.

I nod. "I assumed she'd have heard from someone, or looked at the website or something. It's not like we hide the information from anyone."

"Did you look her up?" Dad asks.

"What? No. Just the file you gave me."

"Then isn't it fair to assume she did the same thing?"

His words sink in. When Dad introduced me to her, he just used my first name, and we've never had a reason to talk about my surname. "This is all my fault." I sit on a stool and hide my face in my hands.

"Yes, it is," Dad agrees.

I look up sharply.

He shrugs. "What do you expect me to say? If you think it's important that a woman knows who you are, then tell her. If she knows already, no big deal."

"That's not great advice now, Dad," I point out. "It's a few dates too late."

"How serious is it?"

"I don't know. But I feel like she could be it for me."

Surprise flits across Dad's face. I can't say I blame him for his reaction. It's not that I've been one for meaningless flings, but I've also never really been in a particularly serious relationship either. There just hasn't been time with my career to consider.

"All right, then you need to go and explain to her," Dad says.

"I know. But what can I say?" Somehow, I don't think *sorry I forgot to tell you who my dad is,* will do the trick.

"The truth. Always the truth. The number one rule about women is to always tell them what you really mean. Unless they ask you how they look, then the answer is always *beautiful*."

I shake my head in bemusement. "Is that what you do with Mama?"

"Yes. Now go and fix your mess," he instructs.

Technically, it's his mess. If he hadn't offered Hazel a job, the fact I'm his son wouldn't have come out like this and I wouldn't be in so much trouble. But it's best not to mention that. At the end of the day, I still failed to tell her that I was DeRossi's son, and now I'm potentially going to pay the price.

"I can't go, I have a class starting in ten minutes."

"I'll take it for you," Dad responds.

"Dad..." He has so much other stuff to do, he can't just decide to take a class with no warning.

"I'm serious. I'll take the class, you go and make things right."

"No one's going to get any learning done," I mutter.

"That's on them. They know I run the school, they shouldn't be surprised when I turn up to teach. Now go. And if you can convince her to take the job as well, that would be good."

"Dad!"

"What? She can't be your girlfriend and work here?"

"That's up to her," I point out.

"So don't mess it up." He gestures to the door.

I don't need telling twice and jump to my feet. "Thanks, Dad."

The way he smiles at me makes me think that everything is going to turn out all right in the end. I hope he's right. I don't want to lose Hazel over something like this, not when I genuinely didn't mean to keep it from her.

THIRTEEN

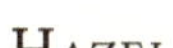

Hazel

How did I miss that he's Antonio DeRossi?

I grab my phone and pull up the cookery school's website. A couple of clicks later and I'm staring at a smiling photo of Antonio in chef whites, his name printed clearly under his picture. There's no denying who he is.

Antonio DeRossi III.

And I had no idea. I've probably even seen his name mentioned in articles and on websites, but considering it's the same as Chef DeRossi's, I've never thought twice about it.

I let out a loud groan.

"What's up?" Rowen asks, setting a takeaway cup of coffee down in front of me. She must have been by Willow's shop.

"You know that feeling when something has been staring you in the face but you still manage to miss it?"

"I do." She sits down opposite.

I pick up the coffee and take a sip, pleased to discover it's a pumpkin spice latte. My favourite.

"What was staring at you in the face?" she asks.

I sigh. "Antonio is DeRossi's son."

"Ah. That."

"You knew."

"And I said as much to you. I looked him up on the website, which I assume is what you've just done," Rowen says.

"Why didn't you tell me?" My frustration comes through my voice.

"I figured you already knew."

"Argh. Why is this happening?"

"Because you didn't bother to search for information on the guy you're dating," she says dryly.

"Yes, yes, it's all my fault. But he could have told me."

"He could have, but he probably thought you already knew. Besides, don't you remember how you felt when Granny first gave us the shop? You didn't like the fact that it felt like you'd been handed something you didn't deserve."

"That was years ago." I'm not sure why she's bringing it up now.

"I know, but you didn't like it, right?"

"I suppose not." Even though I love the bakery, it did used to feel more like we'd been handed something instead of working for it. Since we made some changes to the way things are run, that feeling has mostly gone away, though not completely.

"Perhaps he feels the same way. And then here is a gorgeous witch who doesn't seem to care that he's the son of a famous chef and treats him like she sees who he truly is. If I were in his position, I wouldn't say anything either."

I narrow my eyes at my older sister. "Since when are you team Antonio?"

"I was never against him. I didn't want to see you get your heart broken, and right now, I can see a risk of you breaking it yourself, and that's just as bad."

"I'm not sure what to do, Row."

She places something down on the table next to me. "You put this shot of courage in your coffee, down it, and then go talk to him."

I eye up the shot. The logo reveals it's come from Willow, which means it's trustworthy, but I don't want to take it. Some things should be done without magical help.

"It's okay, I don't need it. I've got this." I take a deep breath. "Do I look okay?"

She cocks her head to the side. "You look normal to me."

"That's not what I meant."

"You look fine," she assures me. "What are you going to say?"

"I have no idea. I guess I'll find out when I see him." I down the slightly-too-hot coffee, its warmth settling in my stomach like a comforting hug.

"Don't you think you should figure it out before you see him?" Rowen's expression perfectly mirrors her question. She doesn't understand how I'm not thinking over dozens of potential conversations in my head so I can pick the best one.

I get why she does it, but life doesn't work that way. I could imagine dozens of ways for the conversation to go, and when it came time to actually talk, it would be completely different.

I'm hoping that seeing Antonio will tell me how I feel about the situation and whether I need to be angry, or if it's okay not to be. I'm certainly a little confused about that part right now, and I want to change that.

"Thanks, Row."

"I didn't even do anything," she mutters as I pocket my phone and make my way towards the door into the shop. There's no time to waste on sorting this out.

The moment I step through, the bell tinkles and a customer walks in.

Except that it's not a customer.

"Hi," Antonio says.

"Hey."

One look at his face tells me that he's realised I was oblivious to his identity and now he's worried.

Clover looks between us, clearly confused about the situation. "What..."

"Why don't the two of you go upstairs and talk?" Rowen suggests from behind me.

I look back to find my older sister giving me a reassuring smile.

"Thanks." My voice cracks, revealing how worried I am about the conversation to come.

Except that he's come to find me as soon as he realised there was a problem. That's a good thing, right?

I gesture to Antonio to follow me and head past my sister. She reaches out and gives my arm a reassuring squeeze.

It's going to be okay. Butterflies flutter in my stomach, but I know they're a little misplaced. Now

I've seen him, I can tell that I don't want this to end, and that this is going to be nothing more than a small misunderstanding that we can talk about.

Hopefully, he feels the same.

I lead him through the kitchens and up the stairs into Rowen's flat, nervous but hopeful about how this is going to end.

FOURTEEN

Antonio

"Do you want anything to drink?" Hazel asks.

I shake my head. Right now, I just need to talk to her.

"Okay, then let's sit." She gestures to a comfortable looking sofa and the two of us take a seat.

We're close enough that we can touch if we want to, but neither of us make the move. We're both well aware of what's hanging in the balance between us.

I swallow down my nerves and open my mouth to speak.

"I'm sorry," she blurts.

I blink a few times. "You're sorry?"

"Yes."

"But why?"

She sighs. "I made an assumption about who you were, or rather who you weren't, and then I built up this whole thing about it and it turns out I'm wrong, and I'm sorry."

"Hazel." I reach out and take her hand in mine, noticing that she doesn't even seem to think about pulling back.

That's a good sign.

"I'm the one who should be sorry. And I am. I just assumed you knew I was DeRossi's son."

"Because everyone knows."

"Well, yes. Everyone at the cookery school does. It's on the website, in interviews. And how many Italian chefs have you come across living around here?"

She laughs slightly uncomfortably. "I know. When you put it like that, I must seem really dim."

I let out a low chuckle. "We can just tell people that you were distracted by my charm."

"And your handsomeness," she adds.

"That's up for you to decide." I try to resist the urge to beam with pride at her compliment. It means a lot that she thinks I'm handsome. Even more when she's thinking it when she could be mad at me. "Even so, I'm sorry I wasn't more explicit. I should have thought to make it clear."

"It's okay," she assures me. "I felt a little stupid when your dad said you were his son during our meeting."

"Yes, he picked up on that," I respond. "It's how I figured out you had no idea who I was."

"I should have paid more attention." She glances away and fiddles with a thread at the bottom of her dress.

"You paid perfect attention," I counter. "I've never felt more listened to than with you."

"Except that I couldn't work out that you're the son of a chef I've followed for years. I've probably seen photos of you, and then I'm just completely ignorant when I meet you face to face."

"There probably aren't many photos of me." No one really wants to take a photo of the sous chef, especially not when they don't have the same passion for pastry as the chef themselves.

"Your photo is on the website. It's a good one."

"Thank you." So she's looked me up now, good to know. "So, what do we do now?"

"I guess I have to tell your dad that I can't take the job." There's resignation in her voice that I'm not particularly a fan of.

"Why?"

"He probably only offered it to me because he thought we were dating, and maybe you don't want to do that now."

I let out a puff of air, trying to decide whether I need to work on saving us first, or the job offer.

"I still want to date you," I promise. "In fact, why don't you come round to mine for dinner tonight? I was going to ask you anyway, but then all this happened."

She looks up sharply, hope lingering in her eyes. It breaks my heart to think she feared it could be over between us. "You don't want to end this?"

A nervous chuckle escapes me and I rub the back of my neck. "When I was talking to Dad after I found out about the job offer, I told him that I thought you might be it for me. I'm not going to let that go because we both made a slight communication mistake."

"That's a lot to process," she murmurs. "You think I might be it for you?" Her gaze meets mine and I can see a lot of the emotions I feel reflected back at me in her eyes.

"Yes."

"You really think that?"

"I'm not in the habit of saying things I don't mean." Which is something I hope she knows by now, but can understand why she wants to question it right now.

She nods. "Okay. Dinner is good."

I smooth my thumb across the back of her hand. It's not something I've ever really done to anyone before, but there's something pleasantly intimate about it.

"Now I guess we have to talk about the job offer," she says.

"Mmhmm. I'm under strict instructions from Dad not to let you slip away."

"Romantically, or professionally?"

"Both, I think. He's a wise man."

"Except that he hasn't figured out you prefer steak to profiteroles."

"That's an odd combination."

She shakes her head. "I have a croque-en-bouche to assemble, my profiteroles are in the fridge at the moment."

"Ouch, whose idea was that?"

"Mine, and it was a dumb one. I'm having Rowen take it off the website the moment I'm done with this one and making a vow to myself that I'll never make one again."

"I can give you a hand?" The offer is out of my mouth before I can think twice about it. Not that I'm going to.

"I'd say no, but I'm really dreading it. So yes, please?"

"Your wish is my command." I do a small mock bow, making her light up with laughter in the process.

"So your dad *did* only offer me the job because we're dating?" she asks.

"No. He had no idea until after he'd already offered you it."

"Oh." Understanding dawns on her face and she leans back a little. "You mean he actually wants me to work for him?"

"He doesn't offer jobs to people he doesn't want to work with. But I promise, the job offer is completely separate to us. I didn't even know about it until after he'd given it to you."

"Huh."

"Are you going to take it?" I want her to. And not just because it'll be nice to see her at work, but because I think she'll be good at it. From things she's said, I think it's what she's been looking for too.

"I don't know," she admits. "I haven't really had time to think about it, and I don't want to give up working here. I know your dad said that he didn't expect me to, but even giving up a little bit of time is a commitment I need to be sure that I can make."

I nod along with what she's saying. "I get that. I felt the same way when he offered me my first job."

"So you didn't get your job through nepotism after all."

I chuckle. "I think it was a little bit of nepotism. I got offered the job because of who I am, but also because Dad knew I was good at what I did. Like I said, he doesn't offer jobs to people he doesn't want to work with, even if he's related to them."

"Good to know." She lets out a loud sigh. "I feel better."

"For talking?"

She nods. "I know it's silly, but I was so worried about it. I didn't know how I was going to feel when I saw you."

"I'm glad you don't hate me for keeping it from you."

"But you didn't keep it from me," she points out. "You told me several times, I just didn't understand what I was hearing."

"I don't think everyone would share your generous opinion of the situation."

She shrugs. "No one else matters. And for what it's worth, Rowen basically called me an idiot for missing the signs."

"Does that mean she can be my favourite of your sisters?"

"Maybe. But I'll let you change your mind in the future. The others have some redeeming qualities too."

I find myself grinning at the thought of getting to know them all.

Because now we've talked, I'm even more certain of what I thought before. Hazel fits me in a way no one else ever has. She understands what I need and the world I live in, and that's all I've ever wanted.

Maybe with her by my side, I can finally focus on the cooking passions I actually have, rather than those I share with Dad.

A loud ringing fills the air and Hazel lets out a loud groan.

"What is it?"

"That's my alarm to start the croque-en-bouche assembly."

"Ah, definitely groan worthy."

"It is, but at least I have a willing slave to help me with it. Come on, let's get you to work." She gestures for me to get up and follow her back down to the kitchens, which I'll gladly do.

While the croque-en-bouche is going to be annoyingly fiddly and time-consuming, it's going to be time I get to spend with her, and that's never going to be a bad thing.

FIFTEEN

Hazel

Trays of cream-filled profiteroles fill every available surface, while sugar turns to caramel on the stove, and some chocolate work is cooling in the other room. It's a full blown assembly line, and I'm glad I can use Oakley's cupcake room off the main kitchen for it or none of the others would get anything done at all today.

"Ready for the next row," Antonio says.

"Coming." I grab a tea towel and pick up the pan of caramel to take it over to the stand waiting. "Ready."

He nods.

The two of us start dipping profiteroles into the caramel and sticking them into place, working quickly so that it doesn't cool too much and make our job more difficult than it has to be.

Not that it's great to be dipping cream cakes into hot caramel to begin with. Just one of the reasons I hate doing croque-en-bouches. They may look impressive but they always damage the underlying pastry.

"Why couldn't they have asked for a macaron version?" I mutter.

"Is that better?" Antonio asks. "I've never made one."

"I suppose it depends if you like macarons."

"So that's a yes."

I let out a light chuckle. "I think they're preferable, yes. The meringue shells don't need cooking past optimal like the choux pastry does, and they don't need the hot caramel because a blob of buttercream will do."

"A blob?" He can barely contain his amusement.

"Yes, a blob. Which would also be good because I'd be able to put some on your nose when you make fun of my terminology. And then we'd laugh and be cute together."

He glances at the almost empty pan of hot caramel. "Please don't do that."

"I don't plan on," I promise. "I suppose I could break open a profiterole and use the cream, but I spent a long time filling them in the first place, I don't want to waste that."

"Is there any magic in these?"

"Not yet. The client didn't want an emotion because it can't be seen." I resist the urge to roll my eyes. I'm not sure why it matters unless they're trying to use magic as a status symbol, but considering how accessible it is, that seems unlikely.

"Why bother ordering from a witch-run bakery, then?"

"I'm not sure. Maybe they just think our cakes are good? They don't need to be full of magic for that."

"True. So what are you going to do instead?"

"Let me show you." I set down the pan and pull out my wand. "It'll only last for a moment, I'll set it properly once the whole thing is built."

He nods and takes a step back.

I close my eyes and pull an image of twinkling starlight to mind. I don't have to do it to make the spell work, but I think it adds something special to the effect if I do.

I point my wand in the direction of the croque-en-bouche and let the magic tingle through me. It leaps from my arm and latches onto the caramel, making it glitter and flicker even in the harsh light of the prep room.

"That's beautiful," Antonio says, his accent slipping out a little more than before.

I smile widely. "Thank you. It's not a very complicated spell, but sometimes those are the ones that make the most impact."

"No wonder my dad wants to work with you, he could learn a lot."

I cock my head to the side. "Does he not use magic in his cakes?"

"Not really. Nor in his presentation. But I think I'm starting to realise how strange of a choice that is when he's a warlock pastry chef."

"Some people just like to use magic less than others. Or they think it's something private, I don't think there's anything wrong with that." I slip my wand into my pocket.

"You don't think we owe the world our magic?"

I shake my head. "Maybe that's a strange thing to think when I co-own a bakery that specialises in magical cakes, but I don't feel like we owe the world anything. We can choose what we put into it, and what we have to offer goes far beyond the magic we're capable of doing. Some witches will always want to give more, others will want to keep it to themselves. Maybe your dad is one of those." It feels weird to be talking about Chef DeRossi in a more intimate way than before, but I'm going to have to get used to it considering I'm planning on starting a serious relationship with his son.

Who apparently thinks that I'm *it* for him. That should scare me more than it does. Then again, I'm pretty sure I feel the same thing.

We settle back into a workflow, with the croque-en-bouche growing between us. Even though I can think of a dozen better things the customer could have ordered, I have to admit that it looks impressive.

And that it's nice to be sharing some time alone with Antonio focusing on what we're good at. He may have bigger dreams in life than being a pastry sous chef, but it's clear to me how he's gotten so far in his career despite that.

I'm going to do everything I can to make sure I further his dreams, even if that's just trying to find a way to imbibe magic and emotion into the sauces he makes. Who knows where that journey will even take us. For now, I'll be at the bakery and he'll continue as his father's sous chef, but maybe in time, we'll open a restaurant of our own.

I glance over at the handsome chef putting finishing touches to the caramel work and smile.

I can see that. We can create the menu together

and make sure it all compliments each other in the best way. Maybe I can do a dessert of the day so I can get the creativity I need for my patisserie.

They're pipe dreams, and not ones I'm willing to share with anyone yet, but the fact they're even there is making me giddy.

"What are you smiling at?" Antonio asks.

"You."

He chuckles and sets down his pan. He makes his way over to me and pulls me to him with firm hands on my waist.

I wrap my arms around his neck, bringing us even closer together.

"What about me?" His voice comes out as a low rumble, vibrating through me.

"That you haven't kissed me since you arrived and it's a real shame," I respond.

"I'm glad you brought that up." He leans in and my eyes flutter closed.

His lips brush against mine and I melt into him, enjoying the closeness that comes with the kiss.

Someone clears their throat from the door and we break apart.

"Am I interrupting?" Rowen asks.

A flush rises to my cheeks but I look in her direction anyway. "Yes."

She snorts. "Is it ready? The customer is here to collect."

"It is." I gesture to the magnificent creation sitting on the bench. Antonio pulls away from me to start preparing the box for transport while I talk to my sister. It only makes me appreciate him even more.

Rowen nods appreciatively. "It looks good, I imagine you're going to have your hands full with them once photos of this get out."

"If you dare put them on the menu, then I'm going to make sure gingerbread houses make an appearance again at Christmas. Remember how much you hate them?"

"Don't even think about it," Rowen warns.

"Then don't add croque-en-bouches."

"All right, deal. No croque-en-bouches, and no gingerbread houses. Got it," Rowen promises. "Unless someone specifically asks."

I sigh. "Fine. But next time I have one on, I'm calling Antonio in straight away to help and we're paying him."

"We should pay him for this afternoon too," she says. "Otherwise you wouldn't have gotten done."

"That's fine by me," Antonio jokes. "You come work for my dad sometimes, I'll come work for your sisters, it seems like a fair trade."

"I haven't even decided if I'm taking the job yet," I remind him.

"I'll sort it all out," Rowen promises. "And I'll tell the customer that you'll be right out with her order."

"Thanks." I smile at her to assure her that everything is okay and she disappears back to the shop.

"I'm glad you won't have to deal with these very often," Antonio says. "I think it's the first time I've ever helped put one together and I already don't want to do it again."

I let out a light laugh. "Yep, they'll do that to you. Let's get it packed up and then we can go grab some dinner. But I'm not going to make you cook it, that can wait."

He leans in and kisses the side of my head, filling me with a warm glow that I don't think anyone else has ever made me feel.

It's funny how saying yes to a demonstration at my old cookery school has changed so much, but I welcome it with open arms.

SIXTEEN

HAZEL

I'M EVEN MORE nervous about my meeting with Chef DeRossi than last time, probably because he now knows that I'm dating his son and that makes the dynamic a little different from last time.

I knock on his office door before my confidence abandons me.

"Come in," he calls.

I push down on the handle and step into the room.

"Ah, Miss Parkes, what a pleasant surprise."

"I think you can just call me Hazel now," I say.

"Only if you'll call me Tony." There's a knowing

glint in his eye that reveals the truth behind Antonio's statement. He really did tell his father that he thought our relationship could be *the one*.

I try to focus on that instead of the fact that *the* Chef DeRossi just asked me to call him Tony.

"I don't have very long before my next meeting," he says. "But if you want to walk with me, we can talk about whatever you came to ask me."

"Thank you, I appreciate that."

He grabs his jacket and heads to the door. I step back so he can get past and then fall into step beside him.

"I assume you've been thinking about the job proposal," he says.

"I have." I take a deep breath. "I'd like to accept."

He beams widely. "Excellent. Why don't you come in at two next Tuesday and we can have a meeting to discuss how you want the class to be run."

"I get to control that?"

"Of course," he says as if it's a given. Maybe it is. I've only ever taught the one demonstration I did here before, a rolling set of classes is something I've hardly even dreamed of. "I want to make sure the class is rewarding for both the students and the teacher."

"I remember that about my time here. It was before you took over, but even then they took pride in having teachers who loved their craft," I say.

"Which is why I want you on our staff," DeRossi responds. "Who better than to teach people about magical baking than someone with a passion for it and the knowledge to back it up."

A blush rises to my cheeks and I glance away. I'm not sure how I ended up in the position of having the person I've idolised for years speak to me like this, but it's a whole other experience.

"Right, I need to go this way," DeRossi says, gesturing to the left. "But Antonio has just finished a class. Say hello to him for me." He nods towards one of the classroom doors.

He's *definitely* aware that we're together now.

"Thank you for everything, Chef De-Tony." That's going to be hard to remember.

"You're welcome, Hazel. Welcome to the family." He disappears before I can ask him whether he means the cookery school family, or the DeRossi one.

I suppose it doesn't matter.

I pull myself away from the retreating chef's back and open the door. Antonio is inside putting things away, much like he was after the demonstration I gave.

"I'll be right there, D-, oh Hazel. Hi." His face

lights up when he realises it's me coming into the room. "I didn't realise you were here."

"I've just come from talking to your dad," I explain. Perhaps I should have told him I was coming instead of just showing up.

"About the job?"

I nod.

He holds his breath, clearly wanting to ask me about it, but trying to give me a chance to tell him.

I hop up onto one of the benches and swing my legs back and forth, feeling like I'm eighteen again and just starting evening classes for the first time. "I said yes."

His eyes light up. "You did?"

"Mmhmm. Now we work together, you'd better be ready."

"I'm always ready for you."

I let out a soft snort. "That was cheesy."

"But you loved it."

A small smile twists at the corner of my lips. "I did."

"Good, because I have plenty of lines where they came from." He leans against the counter next to me, almost close enough to touch, but not quite.

"I thought Italians were supposed to be masters at love," I tease.

"They are, but they only teach it once you turn

eleven, and I was already here in England by then, so you missed out on the Casanova training."

A loud laugh escapes from me. "It's never too late to start learning."

"It's a good thing I have an excellent teacher then."

"I hope you mean me."

"There wouldn't be anyone else," he promises. "In baking or in love."

"If anything, your lines just got even worse."

"And yet they're still working on you." He grins because he knows he's right. There's something charming about the way he delivers them. More importantly, there's something carefree.

"You know, I've been thinking," I say.

"About?"

"Advantages to working together."

"Oh? And what have you come up with so far?" he asks, his voice lowering. I know what he's getting at, it's the same thing I am too, but I want to tease him a bit first.

"The obvious. If we're working the same day, then we can use one car," I start. "We can have lunch together, that's always nice."

"Mmhmm, good benefits." He moves so he's leaning right up against me. "Anything else?"

I reach out and take hold of the front of his chef's

jacket and pull him closer. Our faces are barely inches apart, leaving very little to the imagination about what I'm going to do. "Why don't I show you?" I whisper.

"I think I'd like that very much."

I lean in and press my lips against his. He reacts instantly, pressing himself against me and placing a hand on my thigh.

I don't waste any time deepening the kiss, enjoying the way it feels to connect to him like this. I've only ever dreamed of being with someone who makes me feel as alive and seen as he does, and I can't wait to explore what the rest of our relationship is going to be like as a result.

EPILOGUE

HAZEL

SIX MONTHS Later

THE KITCHEN LOOKS as if something has exploded, which isn't anything new. The day before Rowen goes to the annual Christmas fayre is always like this. Probably because it has the misfortune of happening on a Saturday too, which is a busy enough day for the bakery as it is.

But right now, the focus is on getting Rowen ready and making sure she has everything she needs, even if it looks rather chaotic.

"Antonio is picking me up in five minutes, if there's anything else you need doing, now is the time to ask," I say.

Rowen spins around and looks between each of the neatly packed boxes in turn. Even without asking what she's doing, I know that she's checking off everything in her head to make sure she has it.

"Did you pack the Christmas pudding macarons? You know I sold out last year."

"I did," I promise. "And if you get down to the last box before three again, then I'll be on standby to make some more and bring them down."

"Does Antonio not mind?"

"Antonio knows that Christmas is big business for us."

"He'll be helping then," she jokes.

"Probably. I haven't asked if he wants to, but the cookery school is closed for the holidays already, so I imagine he will. You know he hates not having anything to do." But he may want to take the time to work on some of his savoury menu ideas to present to his dad for the new restaurant he's thinking of opening. Antonio wants to pitch him a menu in the hopes he can convince his father to finally do it.

"Good, then Oakley won't be alone. You know what people get like around the holidays."

"I do." There are times when all four of us need to be out the front, and we have to haul Ash in to help with deliveries. Not that he seems to mind too much. "Have you remembered to charge the card machine? We don't want a repeat of last year."

Rowen groans. "I knew I'd forgotten something."

"Go plug it in. And don't forget it in the morning." Though one of us will run it down to her if she does. No one wants a repeat of the lost sales not having a card machine made.

"All right. Thanks for the help, Zel."

"No worries. Good luck tomorrow."

"I'll need it." She waves goodbye and heads upstairs to deal with her card machine.

A knock sounds at the door and I turn to find Antonio leaning against it. "Are you ready to go home?"

I nod. "Just let me grab my coat, it's freezing outside."

"That's because it's December."

"I know, I know." I slip my arms inside and close my belt. "All right, let's go."

"Is she all right with all of this?" Antonio asks, looking past me at the piles of boxes left strewn around the kitchens.

"Ash is helping her to take it all down to the

Christmas market tomorrow," I say. "But it's sweet of you to check." I go up on my tiptoes to press a kiss against his cheek.

He turns at the last second, and pulls me closer so he can kiss me properly. I melt into him, enjoying the closeness the two of us share. I thought I'd get used to the way he makes me feel, but that doesn't seem to be the case at all.

I pull back and smile at him. "Come on, let's get home."

He slips his arm around me and I lean into him, glad that I get to spend my days at my family bakery or teaching classes to eager students, and then I get to go home with him.

It's hard to imagine that a macaron cooking class changed my life, but I owe everything to those tiny brightly coloured meringues.

Now they'll always be my favourite.

Thank you for reading *The Macaron Witch*, I hope you enjoyed it! The series continues with Rowen's story, and her adventures at the Christmas Fayre, in *The Gingerbread Witch*: http://books2read.com/thegingerbreadwitch

You can also download a free Broomstick Bakery story here: https://books.authorlauragreenwood.co.uk/npso95j6t1

AUTHOR NOTE

Thank you for reading *The Macaron Witch*, I hope you enjoyed it!

This series was a bit of a surprise to me. If you've encountered the *Eat Your Heart Out* anthologies, then you may know that this book was first published in volume 2. If you're not familiar with *Eat Your Heart Out*, then it's a set of anthologies written by some quirky romance authors. All of the stories are food inspired, and the proceeds were donated to charity.

Each of the Parkes siblings (Rowen, Oakley, Clover, Hazel, and Ash) will have their own story in the Broomstick Bakery series, and their cousin Willow, owner of Cauldron Coffee Shop, has a series of her own detailing her adventures with releasing Azíl from his cursed teapot.

If you want to try making your own macarons,

the recipe Hazel teaches in chapter 2 is based on a BBC Good Food Recipe.

If you want to keep up to date with new releases and other news, you can join my Facebook Reader Group or mailing list.

Stay safe & happy reading!

- Laura

* * *

The Forgotten Gods World

A fantasy romance world based on Egyptian mythology. Each series can be read on its own, but there are cameos from past characters and mentions of previous events.

The Queen of Gods* - Forgotten Gods - Forgotten Gods: Origins*

* * *

The Egyptian Empire

A modern fantasy world set in an alternative timeline where the Egyptian Empire never fell.

The Apprentice Of Anubis

* * *

The Grimm World

A fantasy fairy tale romance world. Each series can be

read on its own, but there are cameos from past characters and mentions of previous events.

Grimm Academy* - Fate Of The Crown* - Once Upon An Academy* - The Princess Competition

* * *

The Paranormal Council World

A paranormal romance & urban fantasy world where paranormals are hidden away from the human world, and are in search of their fated mates. Each series can be read on its own, but there are cameos from past characters and mentions of previous events.

The Paranormal Council Series* - The Fae Queens* - Paranormal Criminal Investigations* - MatchMater Paranormal Dating App* - The Necromancer Council* - Return Of The Fae*

* * *

Twin Souls* - Dragon Soul* - The Renegade Dragons* - The Vampire Detective* - Amethyst's Wand Shop Mysteries - The Necromancer Morgue Mysteries

ABOUT THE AUTHOR

Laura is a USA Today Bestselling Author of paranormal, fantasy, urban fantasy, and contemporary romance. When she's not writing, she drinks a lot of tea, tries to resist French macarons, and works towards a diploma in Egyptology. She lives in the UK, where most of her books are set. Laura specialises in quick reads, whether you're looking for a swoonworthy romance for the bath, or an action-packed adventure for your latest journey, you'll find the perfect match amongst her books!